the INTERVIEW

the INTERVIEW

Patricia O'Reilly

NEW ISLAND

THE INTERVIEW
First published 2014
by New Island
16 Priory Office Park
Stillorgan
County Dublin
www.newisland.ie

PRINT ISBN: 978-1-84840-348-2
EPUB ISBN: 978-1-84840-349-9
MOBI ISBN: 978-1-84840-350-5

Typeset by JVR Creative India
Cover design by Mariel Deegan & New Island
Printed by OPOLGRAF SA, Poland

New Island receives funding from The Arts Council

10 9 8 7 6 5 4 3 2 1

Interview: A meeting of people face to face
– Oxford Dictionary

'There is a dangerous silence in that hour A stillness, which leaves room for the full soul To open all itself, without the power of calling wholly back its self-control:'
Lord Byron, **Don Juan**

About The Author

Patricia O'Reilly comes to writing books via the route of freelance journalism and radio documentaries and plays. She has long been fascinated by Eileen Gray, who is the subject of many of her literary works. Her previous novels, also inspired by real life, include *A Type of Beauty: The Story of Kathleen Newton* (long listed for Historical Novel Society Award 2012) and *Time and Destiny*. In addition to fiction writing, Patricia is a highly regarded creative writing tutor at UCD and elsewhere. She lives in Dublin.

Acknowledgements

*T*hanks to the worldwide fans of Eileen Gray; to director, Mary McGuckian for a part in her wonderful film, *The Price of Desire*; to the Irish Ambassador to France Rory Montgomery for his hospitality in Paris; to the staff of The Princess Grace Irish Library, Monaco; to M. Jean-Louis Dedieu, deputy mayor of Roquebrune for facilitating my visit to E.1027 and to architect i/c Pierre Antoine Gattier for taking me through the villa's refurbishment; to Elizabeth Chatwin for her patient answering of my questions; to the staff at Paris's Pompidou Centre; to Dublin's IMMA and Collins Barracks Museum for the Eileen Gray exhibitions and to Susanne for the scope of her imagination. Thanks too to the editorial director of New Island Books, Eoin Purcell; editors, Emma Donoghue and Sheila Armstrong and all the rest of staff at New Island Books, with special thanks to Mariel Deegan, for the brilliant cover and promotion.

This is for Xavier, Susanne, Peter, Max, Rory and Frank; with love and thanks.

PARIS, 1972

Chapter 1

*T*he Englishman strolling through the November afternoon has the confidence of good breeding and good looks. He passes the Louvre and crosses the Seine at Pont des Arts, looking down in his interested way at the cold green of the river through the wooden slats. Leaving the bridge, he turns right into Quai Conti and then Quai Malaquaise. Lingering along the banks of the Seine, he absorbs the activities and sounds of the Sunday crowds where locals and tourists alike browse the stalls of cheap souvenirs, old books, prints and maps.

By nature he is a collector. He steps up to one of the stalls wondering at the likelihood of finding a rare book, perhaps a century-old signed first edition. It is difficult for him to resist the idea of owning an intriguing anything, especially a book. Many of the tooled leather covers look untouched; more are missing their spines; a few hardbacks have lurid dust covers; but mostly the editions are in the much-handled maroon, green and brown leather he associates with the publishing of books from long ago.

He loves the sounds of words and is in awe of their power; he hopes he is not viewing the selling off of beloved collections.

Old habits die hard. He picks up a copy of *Une Vie*.

The first book he can remember – and at the time he could not have been more than three or four years of age – is *The Flower Fairies*, his memories of it forever etched in association with his mother. Little boy loved. A quiver of excitement would run up his spine each night as he climbed into his narrow single bed, pushed into a corner of whatever bedroom he and his mother happened to be sharing in one of their many relatives' houses. His anticipation was mighty as he waited in his blue striped pyjamas, with brushed teeth and scrubbed neck, his feet warmed by an earthenware hot water bottle wrapped in a fraying towel.

The fragile weight of his mother would cause the side of the bed to creak as she sat, then bent down to slip off her shoes before climbing in beside him. Propped high on pillows and wedged into the narrow space, her settling was fidgety – she was like that then, a nervous, highly strung person, she smoothed down her skirt and she patted at her hair with long, thin fingers.

Finally she would lift the book from the locker, remove the bookmark of his father's latest letter from the war, run the palm of her hand across its surface and only after that little ritual would she begin reading the page she'd finished on the previous night.

Leaning across her, with his head resting on her shoulder, the silkiness of her blouse soft against his cheek and the waft of 4711 Cologne in his nostrils, he would run the pink pads of his fingers across the shiny white pages and over the black words. He knew the words were what told the stories, but he preferred the pictures of the fairies. They wore whispery dresses in the colours of the sugared almonds he got for treats, had fluttering thistledown wings and circlets of daisies in their hair – he knew those flowers were called daisies because Mummy had told him so. Ever smiling and joyous, his fairies stood and flew and sat against garlands of green – young as he was, he wanted to hug happy and keep beautiful close to him.

Despite being a fan of Guy de Maupassant's short stories, he drops back *Une Vie* – he could not bear to own such a sad-looking, ill-treated book. Nothing else laid out on the stalls titillates his interest and, relieved at not having to go through the throes of trying to resist the temptation of acquisition, he turns into the district of Saint-Germain-des-Prés.

Already, at only a quarter past three, the light is turning to the colour of shadowy gull plumage as the clouds grow heavier and darker. He lengthens his stride along rue Bonaparte. It would not do to be late. As always he is aware of his surroundings. He takes in the rich variety of shop-front windows filled with luxurious carved armoires, sofas and tables; jet and amber necklaces, jade bracelets and rings with semi-precious stones displayed on black velvet trays, oil paintings in gilt frames depicting glum but important-looking men and solemn family groups, as well as the domestic bric-a-brac of useless objects – rusty locks and keys, chipped dishes, lengths of oilcloth and the forlorn religious statues so beloved of the French.

Litter funnels along the street: an aluminium can rattles in a gutter and the delicate purple wrappers of fruit trays flutter in doorways. He loves Paris. It is a handsome city, but dirty, he decides, pleased by his objectivity. Cities have their own special smells for him: London is of damp and rotting wood; New York, transformers and electric trains; while the scent of Paris is of garlic and Gauloises.

Solid drops of rain brush his cheeks. Umbrellas sprout like black mushrooms on the narrow street and the heels of women go click-clack on the wet asphalt of the pavement. He turns up the collar of his tweed jacket. Elegantly proportioned eighteenth-century mansions, the aptly named *hôtels particuliers*, are tucked behind high stone walls and equally high wooden gates. He is so deep in thought at imagining the tapestry of living that has been played out behind those gates for more than a century that he almost passes his destination.

The figures two and one – white lettering on a blue background – are high on the right-hand side pillar. The gate is painted the colour he thinks of as Georgian green and is dominated by a sturdy knocker. There does not appear to be a bell. He lifts the clapper of the knocker and brings it down sharply against the base. Once, twice, three times. The sound reverberates throughout the unseen courtyard. Running his fingers through his hair – he wishes he had thought to bring a comb – he stands a little back from the gate, shoulders straight and feet planted hip width apart.

With each commission the coil of anticipation in his belly becomes a little more familiar.

*

The woman sits upright, motionless and contemplative, as the day falters and the chill of premature dusk creeps into her soul. For as long as she can remember she has been affected by what she calls her twilight mood: there is something unearthly about day turning to night and light to darkness. Involuntarily she shivers, draws the cashmere shawl more closely around her shoulders and nestles into its warmth. She is compact of body, small-boned and sharp-featured, with dark hair touched with grey, and so determined in all aspects of living that her moments of rest and self-pandering are brief.

With both hands, she grips the curved arms of the chair and eases her body forwards. Settling the soles of her black-laced shoes firmly on the wooden floor, she pulls herself upright, breathing heavily as her distorted fingers grasp at the walking stick propped to the right-hand side of her chair. Ensuring the firm suction of rubber ferule on oak floorboards, she makes her slow way across the room towards the window. Practice has made perfect the sequence of small shuffles that gets her around her apartment.

God's smoky breath, they called fog as children. Standing on their tippy-toes and with noses pressed against the glass, they looked out to the unknown world from the comfort and security of their great house. The family was an abiding presence as, she presumes, families are meant to be: Mama, aimlessly aristocratic, drifting from room to room; Papa, a breeze of energy, the artist of the wonderful homecomings; her brothers, squabbling and fighting, militarily inclined from an early age; and her sisters, craving new gowns and parties and beaux. As children their best possession was youth, but, in the way of the young, it was quite invisible to them. And then there was Lizzie, an all-abiding presence who ensured the household ran smoothly. Housekeeper? Nurse? A bit of both, the family constant and queen of the kitchen, the cosiest place in the old house. She cared for them all but loved her best – 'It's as though you're my own,' she'd say, ruffling her hair or patting her cheek.

She thinks it must be the swirls and wisps of fog that blur the glass and impede her view, although she cannot be sure. For a long time now she hasn't been sure about anything to do with her long-distance sight: she is uncertain of what she sees and doesn't see. She sighs, a whispering sound that leaves a pinprick bubble of spittle on her lips.

Moving from window to drawing table, she rests her cane against its leg. Steadying her body, and with her left hand holding onto the edge of the angled drawing board, she runs the flat of her right palm over the sketch pinned there by its four corners. The cheap brass of the drawing pins glints in the gloom as she reaches for the magnifying glass, grasping it firmly by its black handle. She holds the saucer-sized face to the paper. As she bends down towards the drawing, the lines of her face soften. She moves the device up, down and across the sketch. It is nearly sixty years since first she marked out this preliminary draw-ing, and the charcoal action of the lines and curves, although blurred with time, still has the power to both thrill and awe her.

With a narrow-lipped smile of satisfaction, she leans against the drawing board and looks around her domain. It is her space and it pulses with her creativity, living up to its function of both workroom and salon by fulfilling its purposes and her purposes. She is grateful time has not impaired her memory or her ability to create. Work is what keeps her alive and she is determined that it is by her projects and designs she will be remembered.

The sound of the gate bell cuts into her thoughts.

*

The Englishman follows a bent-over Methuselah type across the small courtyard, the tips of his highly polished shoes squelching through the dampness of the golden and brown leaves scattered over the cobbles. He presumes the old man is some sort of a caretaker, although not, he decides, a particularly effective one, as with every step and wheeze he looks as though he is about to trip over his long, brown coat.

They enter the building through a narrow door with a tapered canopy and step into a hallway with a black and white tiled floor and curved staircase. Turtle-like, the caretaker raises his head. His eyes are red and rheumy and he waits, sniffling and expectant, as the visitor rummages in his trouser pocket and pulls out a fistful of francs.

Money is so unimportant to him that he has little interest in its value, much less an awareness of the rate of exchange in the various countries he visits. He is never sure if an item is too expensive or even unexpectedly inexpensive, but he doesn't have to be concerned about such matters as he has a generously flexible expense account. Yet he enjoys the buying power of money, how it facilitates his travels and can open doors to interesting people.

Suspecting the amount is probably too much for the service he has received, still he passes over the clinking coins and is rewarded by a nod, a half-hearted salute and a wave of an arm indicating the stairs. As he puts his foot on the first step, the retainer holds up his index finger. For a moment he misinterprets the gesture.

'*Merci*,' he calls, smiling as he runs up the stone staircase.

On reaching the first floor, his anticipation mounts as he walks towards the door.

*

At the sound of the outside bell, the woman began her journey back across the floorboards to her chair. While picking at her lunch, her housekeeper had reminded her she was expecting a visitor that afternoon. That was all she had said, and her mistress had acknowledged the information with an almost imperceptible incline of her head and an immediate loss of the little appetite she had for the small fillet of lemon-infused sole on her plate.

So someone would be calling to her apartment. Who was this someone? Why had she agreed to see this person? It disturbs her that she can't recall the purpose of the visit. Perhaps she has never known. That, she is sure, is unlikely. Obviously she hadn't paid attention when the appointment was being set up – that has always been her problem, so she has been told: too wrapped up in her work. She doesn't like visitors, doesn't like being disturbed, doesn't like having any part of her day shaped by outside influences. Her attitude wasn't always quite so, but now it most certainly is.

Along the corridor there is a slow, muffled shuffle followed by an energetic tread. The knock on the door is a firmly knuckled rat-a-tat-tat. Her housekeeper compensates for incipient deafness with noisy gestures, but there is nothing wrong with the woman's hearing. Like her mother before her she can hear a pin drop.

'Yes,' she answers querulously.

As the door opens inwards, she clamps shut her lips and shakes her head in denial; backwards and forwards it rocks on her sinewy neck.

Chapter 2

*T*he woman watches the blurred figure clarify to the shape of a man as it moves towards her. Sentinel-like, the bulk of her housekeeper remains filling the doorway. When the man reaches her chair, he hunkers down, takes her right hand and blankets it between his two. The warmth of his skin surprises her.

'I am Bruce Chatwin,' he says. 'Thank you for agreeing to see me. This is indeed an honour.'

The woman whose hand he holds is Eileen Gray. She is the Irish designer and architect whose work had taken the world by storm from before the First World War and right through the 1920s. Having being forgotten for decades, now, fifty years later, she is back in the international spotlight.

Whoever this tall, slender man is, with the sweep of fair hair over a domed forehead, she hadn't expected the high pitch of his voice. It is the type of educated speech with which she is familiar from her long ago days of socialising in London. Certainly it is not a threatening voice, and he is not a threatening man. But she still doesn't know why he is here or who he is: his name means nothing to her. She nods and he remains holding her hand while her housekeeper dithers in the doorway, her protective indecision swirling out and across the room in potent waves.

'Thank you, Louise,' she says. 'That will be all.'

She knows her housekeeper will be reluctant to leave her alone, particularly with a man unknown to either of them. But no matter how it is between them in private, one mustn't or one doesn't publicly acknowledge a servant's importance. Louise Dany is almost as old as

8

her mistress, although not as physically fragile. Her bulky figure, in its uniform of long dark skirt, loose jumper and rather large feet encased in sensible buckled shoes, projects a sensation of authoritative security. They have been together for nearly seven decades.

'If you're sure, Mademoiselle?' Louise's English is competent, although her accent is thick.

Bruce straightens up, lets go of Miss Gray's hand and turns around. 'Don't you worry. I shall treat your mistress like the rarest piece of Ming porcelain.' He ignores the housekeeper's look of stony incomprehension.

When the door closes behind Louise, Miss Gray realises her vulnerability. It's not that she doesn't feel safe with this Mr Chatwin – there is nothing intimidating about him – but she does not want to be alone with him. She doesn't ever again want to be left alone with any stranger.

There is a dryness in her throat and her heart is thumping. She is not panicking; she will not panic; she never panics. But where the hell is that little bell? Even though she seldom uses it, she likes the feeling of security it imparts and the knowledge at how speedily the ear-splitting sound of clapper against brass can still bring Louise to her side.

Her hands ruffle the air.

The bell should be there on that small table. Louise's constant tidying and moving things from one place to another will be the death of her.

'What is it?' Bruce asks.

'Nothing.'

'What are you looking for?'

'I am not looking for anything.'

Bruce ignores his hostess, bypassing her denials as though she hasn't spoken. 'Can I get you something?' He is again looking down at her.

'I said no. Absolutely not. You cannot.' She is aware of the tone of irritability in her voice and points to the chair on the opposite side of the fireplace. 'Please sit down and tell me why you are here. I do not have much time today.'

All she wants is to order him to go, to leave her be. But something has stopped her. She is uneasy at not being able to identify this something. Could it be a new indecisiveness? She hopes it's not the same sort of vagueness and dithering that afflicted her mother towards the end of her life. No, the *something* that had her inviting him to sit was his voice and charm, and her curiosity; she may as well admit it.

Charles Bruce Chatwin, who is young enough to regard himself as impervious to shock, is shaken to his core. He had not thought of Eileen Gray as being old, although from his research, of course, he had to have known. But from photographs he has seen of her projects, the energy, freshness and timelessness of her work had assailed him in waves. As he had grown more and more fascinated by her and her achievements, the implications of her chronological age became so unimportant that it hadn't registered with him. She was born in 1878 which means she is now ninety-four years old. From the look of that black patch she cannot see out of her right eye, and the other lens in the heavily framed tortoise-shell eyeglasses is bottle-end thick.

He is genuinely fond of and has an affinity with old people. He was a war baby, growing up with his mother in the company of his grandparents and great-uncles and great-aunts, as well as a selection of near and distant elderly cousins. His father was part of that war. A vital part, he knew, being schooled from an early age in accepting that because his father, the captain, was such an important war hero he was seldom able to be home.

Bruce believes in the power of first impressions and they have seldom let him down. From his first glance, Miss Gray's sense of individuality reminded him of his grandmothers, both quite outrageous in their own way. But second and subsequent glances confirm that, despite the three women sharing this quality of uniqueness, Miss Gray is quite different. His grandmothers were outgoing and had an aura of personal confidence about them, while he senses a touch of the introvert about Miss Gray.

'I am still waiting to hear why you're here.' Her voice is premonitory.

'I particularly wanted to meet you.' He hopes his answer doesn't sound lame. Her attitude does not invite explanation, and his instinct whispers it would be better not to elaborate on his credentials at this stage.

'Why did you want to meet me?'

'Well … Because of the work you've done –'

Without waiting for him to finish his sentence, she interrupts. 'What have you seen? What do you know of my work?'

'To answer both of your questions, not as much as I would like to.' To his ears, his tone of voice lacks conviction. If he isn't careful he'll find himself being escorted back across the courtyard by Methuselah. 'But, please, allow me to explain.'

'Please do.' One must have an explanation.

'I've come especially from London, hoping to hear from you about some of your projects.' For now, he won't mention the word interview.

'I am certain I did not agree to see you …?' Her voice drifts off. Damn it, she cannot be sure.

'It is my understanding that you did.' Bruce is a recently appointed feature writer with the *Sunday Times* Magazine. His interviews in Paris that weekend were set up by the editor's secretary who, despite her outlandish clothes and outrageous eye makeup, is efficiency personified. Yesterday he had spent the morning with couturière Madeleine Vionnet without problem. As he hadn't heard to the contrary, he presumed the two hours he had requested with Miss Gray had been agreed by her.

'It is well known that I refuse to see strangers.'

Having spoken, Miss Gray clamps closed her lips, pursing them so tightly that they disappear into the folds of her chin. This Mr Chatwin doesn't appear to her to be the type of man who makes untrue assertions but one cannot be too careful. Since what those damn newspapers and magazines keep calling her 'rediscovery', strangers have become the bane of her life, particularly those pushy and demanding reporters who behave as though they have the right to expect her to supply answers to their outrageous questions and adopt ridiculous poses for their photographers. 'And I refuse to talk to reporters,' she adds.

Bruce now knows at first hand what that cliché of a dropping heart feels like, but his comment is automatic and soothing. 'Of course you do.' He spreads his hands in a disarming gesture. 'It is quite understandable.'

She looks sternly at him out of her good eye. 'You had better give me a proper explanation of why you are here, and pay me the courtesy of doing so quickly.'

Bruce Chatwin is a man rich with charm and easy with grace. When the necessity arises, he is a master at fabricating plausible reasons and excuses. After a quick consideration of the current circumstances, he decides skirting the truth is his best option for the present. He is touched by Miss Gray's feisty vulnerability, touched to the point of feeling protective towards her. She has a resilience that has him aching to capture her spirit in words.

Leaning towards her, he speaks slowly and clearly. 'As you must be aware, the sale of your screen – the Destiny Screen – has resulted in much conjecture. When I carried out some research on you – because I was both curious and interested – I became fascinated with both you and your projects, particularly the screen.'

As he speaks he watches for her reaction. He uses his charm quite consciously and as a social tool, and he is used to eliciting positive responses from the people he meets. But Miss Gray's expression remains bland, sphinx-like. It's as though she hasn't heard what he's said, and if she has, she isn't interested. Refusing to be put off, he continues, 'Even though I'm not familiar with all of your work, I am aware of several of your pieces.'

Until a few weeks ago, when Yves Saint Laurent's agent had pushed up the bidding to $36,000 for the Destiny Screen at an executor's auction of Jacques Doucet's estate, the screen and its designer had been long forgotten. When the story of the record-breaking price for a 'modern' antique made the international newspapers, it was followed by reports on radio and television, and the news-hungry world clamoured for detail. Detail didn't disappoint.

Originally the screen was bought by Jacques Doucet, the internationally renowned couturier who dressed the crème de la crème of the Belle Époque generation, and who was equally famous for his discerning collection of Art Deco, with the screen forming the centrepiece.

Initially it was believed the screen's designer must be long dead. After all, it dated back to more than two world wars. When it was discovered that it was the creation of a woman who was not only alive and well but still designing, the international media worked itself into a frenzy. Overnight Eileen Gray became a cult figure, with her reclusive tendencies only adding to her mystique. The circumstances surrounding her and her work had captivated Bruce's imagination as he read the newspaper and magazine coverage of the story. Like his other rather obsessive enthusiasms, he knew enough of himself to realise that he wouldn't rest easy until he had met this Eileen Gray and formed his own opinion. From boyhood he has been fascinated by the so-called 'famous'. Breaking down their personal barriers, drawing them out and forming even fleeting relationships with them are the aspects of this job that most appeals to him.

It hadn't been difficult to sell the idea of an interview with Eileen Gray to Francis Wyndham, his mentor on the magazine, whom Bruce has trusted enough to allow him read some of his own unfinished writings.

Since his appointment, the editor's attitude towards him has been one of hostility. Magnus Linklater is a hard-boiled journalist of the old school. From the beginning he made it clear that he was unimpressed by Bruce and sceptical of his ability to interview, write up copy and meet deadlines. With the Vionnet and, particularly, the Gray interview, Bruce is determined to prove him wrong.

However, face to face and with his first-hand experience and understanding of the single-minded stubbornness of the elderly, Bruce fears if he pushes Miss Gray too hard he could alienate her.

As he debates his next move, unexpectedly she says, 'Yes, indeed. My pieces. And which pieces, may I ask, are you familiar with?'

Settling into her chair, she starts dragging a small grey shawl over her knees, patting and fussing with the fine wool in an effort to spread it evenly. She is elegant in a silver V-neck sweater over a white silk blouse closed at her neck with a curling golden brooch. He appreciates elegance.

He makes to rise. 'Can I help?'

'No. Not at all. I can manage.'

He watches her excruciatingly slow fumbling, waits until she seems satisfied, and then, with steepled hands, he leans towards her. 'I'm particularly interested in the Destiny Screen. I'd love to know the story behind its creation.'

She raises her head and, with a half smile, looks directly at him. 'How do you know to ask that?'

'Because, I understand, it's the piece that originally brought you international attention and recognition, and it has done so again.'

She won't let him know how impressed she is at his use of the word 'creation'. From start to finish the screen was a creation. 'Had you not heard of me or my work before the recent auction?'

There is defencelessness in the tone of her question. Despite her star being in decline for decades, at the height of her fame she would have been used to interviews, photographic sessions and being the centre of attention. She should be *au fait* with the flimsiness and unpredictability of fame and publicity. After all, rather like riding a bicycle, it's not something you forget. Yet she appears to be oblivious to the fact that her present rush of fame is solely due to the publicity garnered by the agent of a world famous couturier bidding up her screen to a record price.

The only reason Bruce is with Eileen Gray in her apartment is to turn an interview that he plans to handle as an informal chat into a publishable profile with the aim of throwing new light on her and her projects for the magazine's readers. 'In-depth' and 'personal' were Mr Linklater's parting cautions. Bruce should tell Miss Gray why he's here, make sure she understands. It is unethical of him not to do so. But he can't bring himself to. Not yet. Perhaps she'll remember of her own accord. After all, the appointment wouldn't and couldn't have been made if she hadn't agreed to being interviewed.

He believes Miss Gray's apparent hostility is not directed towards him; he hopes it is no more than the reluctance of vulnerability. Given enough time, he is sure, he will be able to draw her out, but he also knows it will have to be done carefully. With Ming porcelain care.

'No, before the auction I hadn't really heard of you,' he prevaricates truthfully.

'I thought so. At least you are honest. Many of the people who come here pretend to know all about my work and myself. Reporters are the worst. They believe that with a bit of research, as they call it, they can pull the wool over my eyes.'

After that burst of forthrightness, Bruce is even more certain he cannot yet own up to being one of that despised breed. He will tread cautiously and carefully, try to build a relationship while regarding and treasuring each second in her company as a bonus. 'As far as I know, from about the thirties there hasn't been much coverage of you or your work,' he says tentatively, 'but now that you have all this publicity, your rediscovery must be exciting?'

The majority of the people he interviews relish the opportunity to talk of their successes and ambitions. But once he has said 'publicity' and 'rediscovery' he realises he has met someone to whom not only the words but also the concepts are immaterial.

'No,' she says, 'my rediscovery isn't at all exciting, but the creation of *Le Destin* was one of the most exciting, rewarding and interesting things that ever happened to me.'

He remains silent, trusting she has forgotten that he has stalled on answering her question as to why he's here, hoping she will elaborate on the screen, wondering will she talk freely. From experience he knows that silence can be an effective trigger for information. Despite the gurgling of water from the radiator in the corner and the flickering flames of the coal fire, the room is still and quiet and chilly.

Miss Gray doesn't disappoint him.

'I believe my life began with the creation of *Le Destin*.'

Chapter 3

Strictly speaking, the life that Eileen Gray sought for herself began in 1907 when she succeeded in making her home permanently in Paris. But over time she has become so enamoured and intrigued with her Destiny Screen that she has developed the habit of saying, and indeed believing, that the screen was the catalyst.

And in many ways it was.

She explains to Bruce how as a young woman she had fallen in love with lacquer-work. After years of taking lessons and honing her skills on small pieces, she had emerged from the chrysalis of an arduous apprenticeship determined to stretch her talent to its limit by creating a special piece. The year was 1912. The sinking of the unsinkable *Titanic* was reverberating throughout the world, and there was a do-or-die attitude in Europe. In Paris this attitude was assertive and particularly associated with the arts. For Eileen and her friends, the liner's sinking reflected the transience of life and the importance of *carpe diem*, as they would say with a gay wave of their hands.

· 'I wanted to work on a large lacquer piece, create something allegorical or mythological, or perhaps a blend of both,' she tells Bruce. 'I loved the medium of lacquering.'

'So you were about to create a statement piece?'

She smiles thinly. 'That wasn't quite how I thought of it. But back then it took me so long to find my subject that I had plenty of opportunity to dream the dream.'

Up to the time of her decision to branch out with her own design, her teacher, the talented Japanese lacquerer Seizo Sugawara, a perfectionist and a hard task master, had restricted her to working on small panels. From experience he knew that the movement from small to large pieces of lacquering was as much psychological as physical, and it was something not easily achieved by even the best of pupils, such as Miss Gray.

Aware of his attitude, Eileen kept silent about her plan. For months she searched for her perfect subject – convinced that when she found it she would instantly recognise it. In high moments of hope, she believed it might present itself to her as she went about daily life, sketching and painting in the various art classes she attended, working with Sugawara, wandering the streets, or on the many sleepless nights when she gazed out of the window looking to the star-studded sky for inspiration.

But it didn't.

In the end, she and her subject found each other, and it happened when she least expected it.

On one of those warm, breathless August afternoons typical to Paris, she took what she used to describe laughingly as one of her 'aimless perambulations'. During these solitary walks which could last for hours, she browsed and absorbed the charm and industry of the small warren of streets that criss-crossed her beloved 6th arrondissement. Her saunter on that occasion followed its usual pattern until an unexpected shower of rain drove her to seek shelter in a narrow door-way which led to a small gallery.

She glanced around the walls at the pictures, her eyes professionally skimming and assessing before being drawn to and held by a simply framed pen and ink drawing locked into a shadowy corner. Blinking in the dim light, and with her nose almost touching the glass, she was just about able to make out the figure of a man. There was something about him that held her attention, and she was enveloped with certainty that he was reaching out towards her. Without knowing how or why, she was certain his message was one of sadness and loneliness. The picture was unsigned, but it was dated July 1882.

'Do you know who did this?' She turned around to ask the only other occupant of the gallery. He was an emaciated-looking student type, with greasy hair and adenoidal breathing. His easel was propped in front of a painting of a peaceful river scene which he was interpreting with a series of heavy linear slashes. His disinterest in her question showed in his shrug of dismissal. 'Do you know anything about it?' she persisted.

'It's said he was a madman incarcerated in La Salpêtrière hospital.' He turned his back firmly on her.

The shiver that ran up and down her spine had nothing to do with the dampness outside, the coolness of the interior or its solitary occupant. She had found her inspiration. With every fibre of her being she knew she had a focus that would facilitate mythological interpretation with a touch of the allegorical. Already she could envisage the blurred outline of her completed project.

As she sat in the gallery's only other chair, with her notebook resting on her navy-skirted knee, ignoring the sticky cotton dampness of her blouse across her shoulders, she sketched a quick likeness of the drawing. The humanity of the man's insanity and his pain touched her emotions so intensely that she had to blink fiercely to prevent tears from spilling down her cheeks. For a long time – ever since her father had left the family home – she had fought against any form of emotionalism, considering crying to be a sign of weakness. But in that small gallery on that damp afternoon she was filled with a new certainty that the senses never lie and that by following her intuition she was, at last, en route to creative fulfilment.

After all the months of searching, in the same way as she had found her artistic milieu with lacquering, she had found the subject for her debut proper.

Once she got started on the project she was certain the internal creative jangling that had her so agitated and uneasy would be soothed and calmed. It never crossed her mind that the work she was about to embark on would herald the beginning of her international recognition.

For more than seven decades, she has allowed her creativity and most of the decisions she has made about her life to be driven by instinct, an instinct that when adhered to has never failed her.

By the time Eileen emerged from the gallery, rain had given way to sparkling sunshine, but her head was so reeling with ideas and images that instead of wandering back at leisure to her apartment, she ran all the way, brushing past pedestrians with an apologetic *excusez-moi*. She was dithering with impatience to get to her easel, but that afternoon the pavements seemed to be thronged with people determined to impede her progress.

'Sugawara-san, Sugawara-san! Where are you?' She burst into the apartment, pulling off her gloves and removing her hat, which she dropped onto the armoire, but she kept, held between her teeth, the precious piece of paper on which she'd sketched the images of the figures.

'What is it, Mademoiselle? What is it?' Louise emerged from the kitchen, her face red and her hands floury.

'Where's Sugawara-san?'

'He's in the bathroom.' Louise sniffed and her tone dropped into disapproval. Since her mistress had persuaded the Japanese man to take her on as a pupil, he treated the apartment as his personal workroom, scattering sketches, brushes and pots all over the place and appropriating the only bathroom, which was constantly filled with steam running down the walls, across the ceiling and puddling on the floor. Even though Miss Gray had leased an atelier for lacquering, she and the Japanese did much of their work in the apartment.

Seizo Sugawara came along the corridor with an angled lacquer brush in his hand. He was a small, slender figure of a man, with clipped black hair falling over his forehead, weary eyes and a soiled apron.

'Yes ...' He inclined his head slightly.

'I've found something wonderful. It's what I've been looking for.'

'In a moment, please.' He never allowed his placidity to be ruffled. His expression was deadpan as he turned back into the fuggy bathroom. He was on the tenth coat of lacquer for a small black cabinet Miss Gray had commissioned as a gift for a friend.

Louise returned to the kitchen and Eileen followed Sugawara.

She perched on the edge of the bath, breathing the thick moist air. Squatting like a child, holding the flat brush in his right hand, meticulously and with the barest movement of his wrist, Seizo Sugawara applied a thin coat of lacquer to the back of the cabinet, simultaneously managing to rub it in and avoid the markings of brush strokes. His silence and the sensation of stillness surrounding him were total; as always his attention was of the present, completely on his task.

As far as Eileen could see there was not a blemish on the gleaming smooth blackness. From personal experience she knew it took time, painstaking training, practice and more practice to gain such expertise. She knew also that in her teacher's opinion she was still a raw apprentice, but she was confident that she was ready to move on. As conflict wasn't in Sugawara's nature, she suspected he wouldn't agree but she was equally certain he wouldn't argue.

'When you're finished with that, we'll have a glass of wine,' she said.

Sugawara's brushstrokes didn't falter but he raised his eyebrows and nodded. It had been a long, arduous day. He would be glad when it ended. It would take about seventy-two hours for this coat of lacquer to dry and only then could he rub it down. By his reckoning the piece would need another two coats to reach the gleaming perfection he sought.

When he joined Eileen in the salon some half an hour later, early evening sunshine cast a golden glow around the carafe of wine and the two glasses on a tray on a table in the centre of the room.

His pupil was standing in front of her easel. From the hunch of her shoulders and the spread of her feet, he recognised the signs: her visual inspiration was on feverish boil. That was the trouble with Europeans. They didn't have the placidity and the calmness of nature that made his countrymen, particularly those like him from the village of Jahoji in northern Japan, the undisputed world masters of lacquering.

While he watched, she tore off a sheet of paper which she crumpled and threw to the floor. Without turning around, she acknowledged his presence with a wave of her left arm.

In broad, determined movements, she started over again on another sheet of paper, blocking out figures, her stick of charcoal moving swiftly across the expanse of white sheet. She appeared to be driven by a new and creative energy. From the months he'd spent working with her, he suspected she was afraid to stop for fear she would lose the momentum to capture the mood of whatever subject she was pursuing. She was edgy when she had an idea. With a few lines, the shape of a slight youth emerged; the next figure was sturdier, probably older. He looked as though he were shouldering a body.

The sense of urgency began to leave Eileen's body and she stepped back in assessment. Despite it being only a rough draft, the dark shapes on the white paper had emerged as powerful figures, yet at the same time they appeared to project an underlying helplessness. A whisper of breath escaped from between her lips and she pushed a strand of hair behind her ear.

'Well, what do you think?' she asked turning around.

Of old, Seizo knew her question to him was merely a courtesy. But on this occasion he was impressed by the vitality of her sketching, although whatever he thought or didn't think would play no part in what ultimately his pupil would decide. She gave the impression of being quiet and gentle, and she was a perfect lady, a generous payer too, but, as he had discovered to his cost, she was as determined as any man and possessed a will of iron.

'Interesting,' he said cautiously, which was high praise from him.

He wasn't sure if the sketch was an end or perhaps a beginning. Lacquer rash was irritating his hands and arms, his eyes were smarting from the mixture of steam and fumes and his body ached from the tension of long hours working at such awkward angles in the confined space of the apartment's minuscule bathroom. He wanted nothing other than to return to his room, eat a little rice and sleep.

'I see it on a screen about so high.' Eileen stood back and measured upwards – at least four feet.

'A panel,' he corrected.

'No. Four panels. It'll be a four-panelled screen.' She tapped a stick of charcoal against her lips.

With a gasp of astonishment at her audacity, he realised Miss Gray was looking for his approval to start on a project that would cause the lacquer masters back in his village to shiver in their slippers. What could he say? Work may be the oil of the soul but it had to be tempered with reason.

21

'You're setting out on a formidable task.' His voice was low and firm. As her teacher he felt it was his duty to warn her of the immensity of what she was considering. 'It will be a very large screen, and it will take you many months to complete.' From his twelve years of living in Paris, he knew Europeans did not have the patience of the Japanese.

'I'm tired of working on small pieces.'

Anxiously his head bobbed up and down. 'Traditionally that's the way we lacquer workers hone our skills.'

'Yes, I know. You've told me again and again, and I've served my apprenticeship on all those small pieces. I know I'm ready to move forward.'

For a moment Sugawara wondered if she was dismissing him. It wasn't easy finding employment. He had first come to Paris for L'Exposition Universelle of 1900, fallen in love with the city and never returned to the austerity and poverty he'd grown up with. Despite the popularity among the wealthy of Paris for simple pieces of lacquer work, there were few commissions and still fewer outlets for his skill as a teacher. He was lucky to have Miss Gray as a pupil. She was one of the typically aristocratic and moneyed Europeans who had made Paris their home, but, demanding and lacking in humility as she was, working with her ensured he ate, kept a roof over his head and each month was able to send back a little money to his family.

'Of course, you'll have to help me. Well, not really help. More confirm that I'm doing everything right. This time I want to be able to say I've done all the lacquering myself.'

'Have you thought of colours?' He may as well humour her. No matter how he protested, he knew her well enough to realise he wouldn't succeed in getting her to change her mind.

'Red, I think. And blue, I want to use blue.'

'Blue is impossible.' The negative burst from him. She knew that – she had brought up the subject of blue on many occasions. Because it happened to be her favourite colour, she insisted it had to be a feasible lacquer colour. 'The great master lacquerers have never succeeded in finding a solution for creating the colour blue.' Now he spoke quietly, firmly and factually. He had already told her the same thing many times previously, but she refused to accept such limitations: he would never contradict her outright.

She clucked in disbelief and ran her fingers through her thick chestnut hair which she had loosened from its clipped confines. 'Well, I believe I might have found a solution. I've been carrying out some experiments that are beginning to prove successful.'

He nodded. He would leave the subject of blue alone. It had him worn out. Disagreeing with Miss Gray when she had hold of one of her theories was a waste of time.

'And the back of the screen will have to have a focus of interest too. Something abstract, I think. Perhaps swirls.' She was alive with anticipation; her voice was clipped crystal and her confidence total.

'A piece that size could require up to thirty coats of lacquer, maybe even forty,' Sugawara tried again, considering it his duty as her teacher to alert her to the drawbacks of such a project.

'Absolutely. If thirty or forty coats are what it takes, then thirty or forty coats are what it will get.' Eileen handed a glass of red wine to Sugawara. He waited while she poured another for herself. 'Here's to my screen. *Slainte.*' She raised her glass towards the drawing board.

Ever watchful, Seizo took a delicate sip. His employer was a realist which, he supposed, helped. As he had discovered, she was a hard worker too. But she had no need to earn money and that, he considered, could be a disincentive to putting in the months of arduous work that such a project would demand.

He wondered would her creative drive and enthusiasm be strong enough to ensure her completion of the screen.

Chapter 4

'You have no idea of the all-consuming passion that coursed through my veins during the months I spent creating the screen.'

Miss Gray leans slightly forward in her chair towards Bruce as though to emphasize what she's saying. She has enjoyed recounting the story of her screen without interruption. Despite her aversion to callers, she finds she is not averse to whiling away a half hour or so with this courteous young man who reminds her of the beaux of her youth and is so interested in her work. It has been such a long time that she has quite forgotten the joys of an appreciative audience.

'I can only imagine,' Bruce tells her quietly.

Despite his interest in what she is saying, he is feeling uncomfortable, tight and buttoned up at being the recipient of her memories under what he considers to be false pretences. And now there's the added disturbing matter of the presence of a cat.

Anxiously he watches as a large black tom uncoils from a bundle of drawings, languidly stretches before it stands up and, with tail erect, pads across the room. Towards him? He hopes not. He is a man without strong dislikes but since his childhood run-ins with his grandmother Isobel's cat – a large, ungainly specimen called Monty who scratched and spat at will – he not only dislikes cats, but he is nervous of them.

'Puss, puss,' Miss Gray calls, stretching her arm towards the cat. With a throaty purr the animal settles on her shoes – highly polished, Bruce notes with approval. Ridiculous as it may be, he has a habit of judging people by the care and shine of their shoes. Like father like son? The captain always insisted on gleaming footwear.

As well as having the worry of a cat in the room, Bruce is trying to remember verbatim what Miss Gray is saying. Ever optimistic, he is hoping for the miracle of a change of mind. Hers. So that he will be able to capture on paper her essence as a woman and a designer, as well as the vitality of the atmosphere of the apartment. His moleskine notebook has to remain firmly in his pocket until he has her agreement for him to carry out his interview. If ever. Thanks to his almost photographic memory, he has no need to refer to the questions he has prepared.

From the time he was a young boy he has been a collector of objects and an originator of atmospheric spaces. As she talked about finding the source of inspiration for her screen and Sugawara's attitude to her project, his imagination took over: he created the settings – the streets, the Parisian rain and the gallery; saw the players: the inept artist Louise, Eileen and Sugawara-san; heard their dialogue and wallowed in the richness of the story which pulsed for him in three-dimensional colour. The only interruption in its unfolding was when he paused to highlight, mentally, an occasional key word or phrase.

He is fascinated by Eileen Gray's room, the womb of creation for her projects: the high white walls with an occasional painting, large worktable, rolled up bundles of drawings propped against the corners, various squares, rectangles and triangles of wood, dusty glass-encased plywood models of some of her projects and everywhere samples – swatches of leather and tweed, rods of chrome, strips of plastic, panes of glass. Here he is surrounded by a lifetime of her imaginative living and the resonance of all that creativity still lingers, present in the very air he is breathing. But as far as he can see there is no evidence of personal mementos or photographs.

His interest in collecting began while he was staying with Grandma Isobel, his father's mother and a Justice of the Peace. From the adult conversations he eavesdropped on at every opportunity, he picked up a most interesting kernel of information about what being a Justice of the Peace meant: if the Germans invaded England his grandmother had the power of execution. Ghoulishly he imagined how she'd go about this executing: Chopping off heads? Shooting through hearts?

Hanging? Then he'd think about the excitement of his grandmother and father between them winning the war.

During his times at Dronfield one of his greatest pleasures was to steal into the dining room to gaze at the cabinet. The cabinet in question was Victorian, a solid mahogany piece of furniture. The top half could be lifted off and there were three shelves behind glass doors, and the base was made up of brass-handled drawers. Both shelves and drawers were kept locked, and his grandmother used them as a depository for carefully labelled family mementos. These items were a trigger for Bruce's imagination, fuelling and facilitating his entry into a fantastical world of all sorts of adventures in exotically named places – his equivalent, he believed, of Narnia.

Grandma Isobel's enthusiastic reciting of their history whetted his interest and brought his six-year-old self to the mature conclusion that, since his rightful place in the family had been usurped by the birth of his brother Hugh, 'things' could become substitutes for the affection he felt he was now denied.

His grandmother, who always smelt of Mornay Carnation soap, stood him in front of her while she sat on her special chair; enormous and specially made to accommodate her bulk. Her expression earnest and her voice pitched low, her eyes bored into his brain the importance of what she was saying. 'This piece of red plaid was first worn by Thomas Arbuthnot at the Battle of Sheriffmuir in 1715.' She would pause and purse her lips, the way she did while praying at church on Sundays. 'And the green plaid was worn by Bonnie Prince Charlie in Edinburgh in 1745.' In slow motion, she drew out the words 'Bonnie Prince'.

In keeping with what Bruce sensed was the solemnity of the occasion, he gave her words his complete attention. Young as he was, he realised the way to gain the approval of adults was, first of all, to make sure they knew he was concentrating by standing or sitting without fidgeting and by looking directly at them while they imparted their grown-up information, and secondly, further assuring them of his attention, by a nod and a 'yes' – or, even better, saying something like, 'That's very interesting'. Later he learned to employ, 'I never knew that', together with a smile and a raise of his eyebrows.

It wasn't so much that Bruce pretended, but rather he was the kind of child who liked to please. While he only feigned polite interest in the plaids, there was one item – a particularly unusual item – that both fascinated and repelled him. It was a tuft of skin with a strip of coarse red hair attached to it with a pin, which his grandmother stored in a pill box in the back reaches of one of the drawers.

The story of that piece of skin fired his imagination, and he never tired of hearing how it had come into her possession. The skin was from a sloth and it was sent to her as a wedding present from her cousin Charles Milward, who had settled in Argentina. The story handed down through the family was that he had come across the animal when a German prospector panning for gold blew up a cave and discovered, in perfect condition, a giant sloth or *megatherium*. These animals lived during the ice age, weighed in at around five tons and were the size of an elephant.

Never in his life had the young Bruce coveted anything as much as he did that scrap of hairy skin. Its allure was all encompassing. While other boys of his age dreamed of being engine drivers or pilots or running off to join the circus, Bruce grew up dreaming of travelling to Patagonia to meet his Milward cousins and to discover more treasures in blown-up caves.

Lying in bed at night, meticulously he planned his journey, sailing, flying, going by railroad and, if necessary, walking until he reached the city of Punta Arenas which he discovered meant Sandy Point. Perfect.

*

'The sensation of creativity and being creative is wonderful,' Bruce says, 'even the creativity of collecting.' He would like to tell Miss Gray about that piece of skin, like to share those childhood thoughts with her, but he considers such sharing of confidences would be unprofessional. It is unusual for him to even think of opening up to a stranger, particularly an interview subject.

When she inclines her head in what he takes to be a gracious acknowledgement of what he has said about creativity, he knows the time has come to clarify the situation between them. 'I am here from the *Sunday Times* Magazine to write about you.' He has spoken slowly and clearly so there can be no doubt in her mind as to the purpose of his visit. He expects to be asked to leave and he is busy preparing the words with which to plead his case.

Her only reaction is to run the palm of her hand across the shawl that she has spread lumpishly on her lap. The aquamarine stone in the chunky ring on her left hand catches the half light.

She doesn't appear to have heard what he has said, or perhaps it hasn't registered with her. Gaggie, his maternal grandmother, who'd fed him Halibut oil and played with him on the beach at Filey, had ended up a bit like that – sifting through information and absorbing a mere fraction. His mother used to say it was sad to watch her deterioration, as she had been raised in Aberdeen in a middle-class household with a butler. What having a butler had to do with anything, Bruce didn't know, but he remembers her flamboyance, her huge gold earrings, collection of brasses and love of dancing, as well as her skill with the Ouija board and horoscopes and gambling.

He has done his duty to Miss Gray. He has explained why he's here. No, he hasn't. If she hasn't grasped and isn't actively aware of what he has said, he has not done his duty. On his return from the war, the captain had done a thorough job of imbuing the importance of honour and integrity, as well as polished shoes, into the lives of his sons.

'Miss Gray, I'm here to do an interview with you,' he says again. There is still no reaction. He speaks considerably louder. 'To interview you for the *Sunday Times* Magazine.'

'There's no need to shout. I heard you the first time.' She rather wishes he hadn't spoken. Now that she knows he's a reporter she has to make a decision about him.

Unsure of how he should react, Bruce shrugs slightly, spreads his hands a little in a rather deprecating manner. 'So is it all right to do this interview? I didn't mean to deceive you. I truly mean what I said about being interested. I hope you'll finish the history of the screen.'

She sighs. For a moment she is unsure of what to do. Those damn reporters are everywhere but this Mr Chatwin seems to be different. He is an English gentleman and she is comfortable with him – she likes the way he wanted to help her with her shawl. It's a long time since she's had such a perceptive listener. And now there's this surge of apologetic, raw honesty from him. She is enjoying the opportunity of retelling the story of *Le Destin*, enjoying it too much to stop. She has always been decisive. She will finish the story. But afterwards, gentleman or not, he will have to go.

'There will be no interview,' she says.

This time she watches closely as he dips his head.

He is still here, he exults. And with every passing minute he is acquiring more information.

In the beginning, when she started on the screen, Miss Gray explains that her waking hours were taken up with filling out the elements from the roughs she'd drawn after coming back from the gallery: sketching the figures to scale in meticulous detail and making sure of the perfection of each curve and line of the drawings.

'By nightfall, I was exhausted, but instead of falling into a well-deserved sleep of creative contentment, I often felt most alive with ideas for interpreting the male forms leaping across fragments of my day.'

Bruce is mesmerised by the passion of her storytelling. How, of his own volition, the naked youth whom she had placed at the bottom right-hand corner of the panel seemed to dance off the page as he held out an imploring arm to the older figure, staggering and bowed under the weight of the cloaked corpse.

' I knew the man from La Salpêtrière, as proprietarily I thought of him, was beyond pain, but clothed in a delicately drawn, softly outlined shroud, he regained a modicum of the dignity so cruelly denied him in life.'

Gradually, Eileen translated her interpretation of the activity of her figures: an inanimate drawing became suffused with movement, and the images on her easel shimmered as though pulsating with lives as independent as her own.

When in the middle of one of the most creative parts of the screen she received the unexpected invitation to exhibit at Paris's prestigious Salon des Artistes Décorateurs, she was aware of the honour, especially as it was the first time she had been invited. But as far as she was concerned the pieces of her lacquer work that would be exhibited were in her past. They were finished and done with, and she was absorbed in her present – which was working on her screen.

When rumours began to filter back to rue Bonaparte that her lacquer panels were the most viewed and talked about exhibits in the salon, she dismissed them with a smile and a toss of her head and got back to work. Nor was she impressed at reports of the interest displayed by a certain Monsieur Jacques Doucet, whom she knew as the couturier who dressed the likes of actress Sarah Bernhardt in translucent pastel gowns with lace ruffles. As she favoured the new trend for tailored clothes, the instigator of such furbelows was of no interest to her.

She was unimpressed by celebrity and during the months she spent working on the screen she paid scant attention to world affairs. Germany boosting the numbers of soldiers in its peacetime army passed her by, as did newspaper reports describing the opening of the Panama Canal as 'the greatest liberty man has ever taken with nature'. While she was touched by the death of Robert Scott in the Antarctic and sad for her friend Kathleen Bruce who'd come with her to Paris and married Scott a few years later, it didn't deflect her from her work.

Equally uninformed about the happenings in Parisian artistic circles, she wasn't aware that Monsieur Doucet, whose activities frequently featured in newspapers, was collecting ancient Chinese art and avant-garde modern art for his new Avenue du Bois apartment.

On the Parisian grapevine of gossip she heard that, during one of his many expeditions to the salon, he had admired her *Le Magicien de la Nuit,* but once he had seen her oriental panel, titled in Sanskrit *Om Mani Padme Hum* (Hail to the Jewel in the Lotus), he was besotted by the mood of the piece as well as the theme and workmanship. He had become somewhat of a role model for the aesthete entrepreneur of the day and, as a patron and catalyst, he saw himself as a creative adventurer on the lookout for new talent. Reports back to Eileen confirmed that he was certain he had found such talent in her; reports also added that he was finding her 'annoyingly elusive'.

When he expressed a wish to visit her studio, it was more of an order than a desire, as he was used to his slightest request being carried out as though he had issued a royal command. Being more irritated at the idea of being disturbed than honoured by his interest, Eileen sent a curt excuse that she was too busy to receive anyone. Although, as Monsieur Doucet made it his business to discover, she was obviously not too busy to pursue her interest in aviation, taking flying lessons and being one of the first passengers to fly to Acapulco from Mexico City.

'By then I was well into the project – sometimes I worked in my atelier but mostly I preferred the comfort of this apartment.' Miss Gray looks around complacently. Comfortable is not how Bruce would describe her living accommodation.

Once she had decided to the scrupulous millimetre on the type of wood and the depth, height and width of the four panels, she had the screen made locally. After she finished the screen, she planned to set up a series of ateliers in the area employing craftspeople who would be skilled in the various disciplines she was interested in pursuing.

When she transferred the silhouettes of her three male figures from paper to screen, the colours evolved in a trance-like state of certainty that left her in no doubt. The background was a burnt orange-red of mysterious shadings and shadows; the corpse was a muted grey; the other two figures were a rich blue. Despite Sugawara's scepticism, her painstaking experiments with complicated chemical formulae paid off: she had succeeded in creating blue and, excited as she was with her discovery, she was astute enough to keep the combination of ingredients under lock and key. She finished the front of the screen by highlighting the figures with the merest shiver of silver; on the reverse side she created an abstract composition of vigorous swirls.

Hers was a project slow in execution and long in creation but one which gave her the greatest of pleasures. Sometimes during the small hours of the night, alone in her workroom, lacking sleep, eyes blurring and focusing with difficulty, sustaining herself on squares of chocolate and cigarettes, it felt as if this screen was her life's purpose, as though from birth this had been mapped out as her destiny.

'I was beginning to realise – as Sugawara had pointed out – that to create the perfection I was aiming for required both a physical and mental challenge,' she tells Bruce.

While she was willing to confront both, she hadn't taken into consideration the emotional drain on her psyche. Living a hermit-like existence, she never once flinched from the task she had set herself; she didn't shirk from the time spent refining the smallest detail or the hours closeted in the claustrophobic, steaming bathroom as she built up layer upon layer of lacquer.

Monsieur Doucet bombarded her with solicitous queries as to how her work was progressing. He had heard extravagant gossip about a screen, most of which he dismissed as unfounded rumouring, but still he wanted to be able to say that he had first sight of whatever she was working on.

When she thought about Monsieur Doucet at all, Eileen presumed he was merely using his interest in her lacquer pieces as an entrée to have her as a potential client. Competition between the top couturiers in Paris was intense, and affluent women were used to being courted. She was amused upon hearing how it was well known that she not only had access to a title but also was independently wealthy – how wealthy nobody knew because she remained a mysterious, somewhat reclusive figure, but generally people thought in terms of Croesus.

From the months of her apprenticeship with Sugawara, Eileen knew the application of lacquer was the real skill test of a lacquerer. Days of drying stretched between each coat. In between applying coats came the rubbing down, which she did with a film of charcoal on the sensitive palm of her hand so she could pick up on the slightest imperfection. As the layers of lacquer built up towards completion, the screen took on a further secret life of its own – inwardly enhanced by outward luminosity. It became such a labour of love that she was able to ignore the discomfort of her arms and neck as they became riddled with the ubiquitous lacquer rash.

As her project moved irrevocably towards the finale, she recognised a growing reluctance within her to complete the screen. Would she ever be able to accept it was finished? And if she did, could she bear to part with it? She decided she couldn't, she wouldn't. She would keep it as a sort of talisman. Her creativity, once harnessed, had flowed joyously and, in the end, the technicalities posed little problem.

'One day it was done and even I knew its perfection could not be improved upon,' she tells Bruce, impressed by his attention to what she's saying, with his stillness, interested eye contact and little nods.

*

In the early stages of her creation, she had named the screen *Le Destin*, and now that it was completed she knew had chosen the perfect name. It was the Destiny Screen.

She stood back and inhaled a hot breath of joyous relief.

She exhaled in grateful, lonely slow motion.

It was as she wished, even better than she had envisaged.

Wearing that deep flush of creative contentment, she stretched high and felt smile after smile break out on her lips. But as always she was left with herself and the loneliness of isolation. She would like to have a special somebody with whom to view her completed work. She would like to stand enclosed in affection, with her head resting on a supportive shoulder as she explained the finer points of the screen to that appreciative person.

Her feelings of loneliness are not for sharing.

Chapter 5

*D*espite the storm clouds of war gathering across Europe, Eileen Gray and her screen were the subject of artistic conversation in Paris. Her absence from the rare social functions she usually attended only added to the gossip that swirled about the salons. Not that she minded – she was pleased to give socialising a rest. Unlike the majority of her contemporaries, she disliked what she regarded as the insincerity and commerciality that was the accepted pattern of socialising with artists, writers, architects, poets and interior designers. 'Blowing one's own trumpet,' she used to say with a frown. She considered such behaviour unladylike.

The Duchess of Clermont-Tonnerre, her American lover, Natalie Clifford Barney – who considered scandal 'the best way of getting rid of nuisances', which translated as avoiding attention from males – and Gertrude Stein, Jewish writer, poet and art collector, were dominant forces in the artistic Parisian society of the day. They claimed friendship with the elusive Miss Gray and it was from them that Monsieur Doucet had it confirmed that the project he was so interested in was a screen. A screen? He was even more intrigued. He charmed his various hostesses with inquiries about their health and sent them elaborate bouquets of flowers, in an effort to ensure he was one of the first to hear when this screen was completed.

The morning after he'd heard the news that the screen was finished, and that Miss Gray had been seen dining in Les Deux Magots, he called unannounced to number 21 rue Bonaparte.

The housekeeper opened the door. 'Mademoiselle Gray is not …' Louise began a recitation that over the past months had become a frequently delivered excuse. While she spoke her voice trailed off as she took in the elegant confidence of the unexpected caller who was unknown to her.

'I am Monsieur Jacques Doucet and Mademoiselle Gray is expecting me.' With his air of authority, neatly clipped goatee, pinstriped trousers, grey spats and final man-about-town touch of silver-topped cane he was the picture of elegant sophistication, and he presented the image of a man not to be trifled with. As Louise paused, unsure of how to deal with the situation, he stepped neatly over the threshold, where he stood with an air of expectancy in the hallway.

At that moment Eileen came out of her workroom. Now that she had finished her screen, she had discarded her overalls and was enjoying wearing luxurious fabrics. Although no matter what her activity or what her outer garments were, her underwear was always of the finest hand-stitched silk, preferably in a soft peach colour. She took pleasure in having sensuous perfection nestling against her skin - a sumptuousness that pleasured her and delighted her lovers. That morning she was dressed in varying shades from light blue to navy – a pale silk blouse with a sharply tailored collar under a long, navy, cashmere cardigan and a panelled skirt in a fine wool check. Her hose was silk and her two-tone suede shoes had the fashionably pointed toes and the curved heels of the season. Her newly bobbed hair flattered her classical features.

As this stranger moved confidently towards her, she jerked backwards, feeling like one of those flat wooden puppets worked by strings by street-corner entertainers.

Her reaction to having her privacy breached was instinctively defensive.

Monsieur Doucet's expression of quizzical interest did not change.

She was quietly outraged at the sight of an unknown man in her hallway. Ignoring Louise, she stood regally, looking more through her caller than at him. Her shadow *pas-de-deux* of movement followed by stillness had taken place in a matter of seconds.

She hadn't spoken as she was unsure what to say. But whoever this man was, he appeared to be full of assurance. He lost no time in pressing home his advantage by unbuttoning the pearl buttons and removing his pale grey gloves, his fingers tidily explicit as he rolled the suede and dropped the gloves into his top hat before handing it to Louise.

And then he had the audacity to say, 'After you, Mademoiselle Gray.' He came up alongside Eileen and used his cane as a pointer along the corridor.

'I beg your pardon.' Now she was in no doubt of what to say and her eyes were as sharp as her voice. 'Who are you? What are you doing in my hallway? Louise, what is the meaning of this?'

'I understood from Monsieur Doucet that you are expecting him.' Louise spoke firmly and fearlessly. For the times, mistress and house-keeper had an unusually democratic relationship.

So that was who this strange caller was. Monsieur Jacques Doucet. She should have known. Eileen addressed her housekeeper. 'I am not expecting him. Monsieur Doucet does not have an appointment. You may show him out.' Her tone was imperious.

Unperturbed, Monsieur Doucet interjected, 'I may not have an appointment for today, but you must have been expecting me. You can be in no doubt of my interest in your work. As I am sure you are aware, I have already purchased several of your lacquer panels.'

She looked at him unflinchingly and he returned her look equally steadily until she said, 'I may have heard something of the sort.' By the tone of her voice she sought to show her disinterest in the busi-ness of his purchase of her work, but she suspected that the flicker of awareness in her eyes may have given her away. She hadn't sold enough pieces to be blasé about a sale.

She was in a quandary. She didn't want this Monsieur Doucet in her home. So he had bought some of her pieces and for months had expressed an interest in viewing what she was working on. She didn't want to give the impression of being commercially dim-witted, but she needed him to realise that selling her work was not her priority. Surely that should be obvious?

One couldn't have lived in Paris and been even a reluctant part of its artistic circles without being aware of Jacques Doucet. As the only son of the founder and owner of the successful company that designed, manufactured and sold the Doucet Lingerie brand, he was used to being in a position of dominance and power, and doubtlessly from his success and years of experience in dressing moody actresses, titled ladies and wealthy matrons, he was skilled in conjuring up the right words. But despite his philanthropic good taste, he had come from trade. And with that background one would have to assume he was as commercial as he was creative. Eileen decided he was the type of man who would probably find it difficult to believe that anyone's driving force could be artistic rather than commercial, or that anyone could not put sales and payment first.

Monsieur Doucet stood firmly, determinedly and expectantly, an obtrusive presence, wafting an unexpected faint scent of lavender. Peacock-like, he seemed to preen: straightening his shoulders, raising his head, generally adjusting his elegant body to maximise his height and physique to best accommodate the line of his clothes.

Eileen seldom had difficulty in expressing precisely what she wanted to say, but as she debated the best words to get rid of her unwelcome visitor, he caught her interest when he said, 'I am fascinated to know how you succeed in marrying structure with creativity. It must be very difficult.'

She suspected he was not the type of man to be unnerved or set back by refusal, and he had the tenacity of a dog with a bone. After all he couldn't have built his reputation as one of the most important couturiers of the time, or acquired his various collections of objets d'art, by taking umbrage. She made a sudden decision.

'As you're here, you may view the screen.' Her capitulation was unexpected, almost royal. She was impressed by determination and Monsieur Doucet deserved a reward for his determination, as well as which she seemed to remember he had the reputation of being a connoisseur of fine arts. She ached to have her instincts about her creation confirmed.

She led the way back down the corridor and Monsieur Doucet followed. She pushed open the door and stepped into the room, expecting him to follow, but he remained standing on the threshold. It was as though he was transfixed – face flushed, eyelids fluttering and breathing heavy – and she caught a glimpse of her screen through his eyes: its four panels taking up the centre of the room. With morning light playing across the life-sized figures, the emotional impact of the subject was heightened and acknowledged; there was glory in the execution and a vibrancy of colour. Not only did *Le Destin* dominate, it glowed with an iridescent animation.

Finally he moved. As though in a trance, hands outstretched, he went towards it, reverence in his every step.

'May I?' he asked, his voice a hoarse whisper. She knew he wanted to touch it, celebrate its tactility, the way she had on so many occasions; to run the pads of his fingers across its surface, to trace the figures that were both vulnerable and powerful.

As she watched, from behind the security of her drawing board, she realised she had been holding her breath. She was both amazed and touched by his reaction. She had not expected others to find her screen emotional. Her rather stern features softened as he ran the flat of his palm over the lacquered surfaces. His palm returned to linger on the figure of the young man and he bent down for a closer look.

She had heard of the sorrow of joy, but until that moment she hadn't understood that it could mean the acknowledgement of creative perfection. Without warning, her back curved in suffering, she crossed her hands protectively across her belly and her eyes barely contained their tears: she would ensure they remained contained. Reaching for the handkerchief tucked up the sleeve of her cardigan, she sniffed slightly.

As he looked across at her, she saw admiration in his eyes. The screen was without blemish, better than he would have thought possible, she knew that. She dabbed at her nose and took a deep breath in an effort to put aside her betraying emotions – she had no time for such weakness, although occasionally she would concede that, perhaps, she might be exhausted. She wasn't sure if she'd succeeded in masking her feelings from him.

'What you've achieved is wonderful. Quite wonderful. You must be very proud,' he said. 'There are few artists who could create such a wonder.'

'You wanted to know about its structure.' Her voice emerged strangled. Damn her weakness.

'Well, yes, I did. But now that I've seen it that is no longer relevant.'

She was impressed that he was accepting it on creativity. And she was back in control of her emotions. Technical details would take from the perfection of the completed object. She believed that true creativity did not need explanation, but she hadn't believed that a man such as Monsieur Doucet would be aware of that.

He turned back to the screen, back to look at her. She realised he did not want to leave *Le Destin*.

*

'Did he ask to buy it then?' Bruce asks, wishing he had been there to observe the viewing turning into a transaction.

'Yes, as I turned towards the door to show him out, Monsieur Doucet blurted out something about making me an offer.'

' "An offer for what?" I asked, knowing full well what he meant but wanting to pay him back for his arrogance and presumption, although I was both touched and, I suppose, even a little humbled by his reaction.'

*

Years later, over one of the shared evening meals they treasured, Jacques Doucet admitted to Eileen that even as he mentioned making an offer he was raging at his impetuousness and stupidity. Why had he rushed in saying he wanted to buy the screen? He knew better. He was too experienced a negotiator and purchaser to behave like an amateur. He had intended to work around gradually to expressing his interest in acquiring the piece. Instead he had committed the cardinal negotiating faux pas of showing his hand too early.

From a young age his father had instilled in him the buying ability and power of money, stressing that no one was immune to its persuasion and everyone and everything had its price. Mentally he had calculated: Mademoiselle Eileen Gray was an unknown; with the exception of his purchases, she had sold virtually none of her work and despite having friends in high places, a title and a wealthy family

– he had heard the rumours and gone as far as making his own enqui-
ries – her lifestyle and an apartment such as this were expensive to run.
He could afford to be generous with his offer.

'An offer for your screen, of course.'

'It's not for sale.'

'I beg your pardon?'

'You heard me.' The warmth was gone from her voice. 'I said *Le
Destin* is not for sale.'

It was the first time he'd heard the title. It was too, too perfect.
Now that he had started negotiating, he wouldn't be diverted. 'If it
isn't for sale, why did you do it? Why did you create it?'

'I created it – and for me it was and is a work of creation – for me.
And I did it because I wanted to and I could.' Her tone returned to
imperiousness as she turned towards the open door.

He thought quickly. 'From where do you draw inspiration?' he
asked after her retreating back – anything to hold her interest.

'I beg your pardon?' She twisted around. He had her attention. He
was determined to hold it.

'Your inspiration. From where do you draw it?'

'For what?'

'Your work, of course.'

'Yes, my work.' Bred in the niceties of graciousness, she managed
dismissal without gesture. 'And that is what I should be getting on
with. Now, if you will excuse me?'

He couldn't walk out on unfinished business. 'Please hear me out.
I genuinely wish to make you an offer for *Le Destin.*' Saying the title
confirmed how the mellifluous syllables perfectly matched the finished
object. He could not leave her in any doubt of his interest.

She shook her head irritably. 'It's not for sale. Absolutely not, as
I've already told you.'

*

'He was determined to have *Le Destin*,' Miss Gray tells Bruce. 'He had
decided it was the perfect centrepiece to illuminate the salon of his

new apartment. He had his hand on the edge of the screen, as though by holding on he wouldn't be ushered out. And then he said, "Perhaps I should call on you on another day. After such a large and tedious project you must be exhausted." '

'I was most annoyed at his presumption. "I am not at all exhausted," I told him, wanting to assure him that I wasn't some delicate swooning female. I liked to think of myself as a modern, working woman, but of course at the time I didn't fulfil that criterion. Unlike the majority of working women in Paris I had a generous personal allowance and did not need to sell my work to live well.

'I rang the bell to signal the end of negotiations and summon Louise. "My housekeeper will show you out," I said as I turned my back on him. I positioned myself behind my easel and picked up a stick of charcoal. I presumed and hoped that was the last of Monsieur Doucet.'

Chapter 6

*T*he chilly twilight filtering through the windows of the apartment no longer seems so sad and lifeless to Eileen Gray. Her usually pale cheeks are heightened with a blush of animated colour. It is a long time since she has spoken so freely of *Le Destin* or her first meeting with Monsieur Doucet, and she can not remember ever being quite so open about her emotions.

Her earlier nervousness and feelings of vulnerability at the coming of both dusk and an unknown visitor may have been uncalled for but, in the circumstances, she feels, understandable: she has always tried to make sense of her response to given situations. In all likelihood, the dark current of fear that still flows beneath her creative life dates back to her childhood exposure to the Roman Catholic religion and its preoccupation with tales of those unknown and tormented souls destined to wander for eternity.

Tucked into a corner of the trestle bed in the kitchen, terrified to immobility, she'd listen to Lizzie talking about November, the Month of the Souls and their release from Purgatory. She'd visualise their faceless, unyielding shapes and shiver at the thought of their relentless and unimpeded drifting, lost and alone in the forces of evil. Ever since childhood, she has disliked the month of November.

For decades she hadn't thought about those stories, but in recent times her memories of the darker side of growing up in County Wexford have been powerful, a collage of scariness haunting her throughout the dark hours of night and now beginning to intrude upon the day.

She sits up a little straighter, eases the tightness from her shoulders and by moving her fingers gently she is able to somewhat loosen the cramping in her hands. This Mr Chatwin is quite unique, his looks and personality matching the honey colour of his jacket, the blue of his open-necked shirt and beige trousers. He is gentle, not quite real, she thinks, child-like rather than childish: the kind of a man to whom one wants to give gifts. She is unaware that she is giving him the most precious gift of all: her time and memories.

But he is aware, and he is grateful. He is the instigating trigger and the perfect recipient for such musings. His presence is, as always, both physical and theatrical – much of the thwarted actor he would like to have been still resides within him, and he has learned to use to his benefit his youthful handsomeness and his ability to enchant and enthral. During his schooldays in Marlborough College, he had distinguished himself as an actor specialising in female roles: his Mrs Candour in *School for Scandal* was long remembered.

'So how did the sale of your screen to Jacques Doucet come about?' he asks.

Miss Gray gives a little *hmm*, rather like his grandmother Isobel did on the rare occasions when she recognised she had been outwitted. Nodding as though in affirmation of what she's saying, she speaks slowly. 'He sent a note around saying unless he heard to the contrary he would return on Tuesday morning at eleven thirty. I ignored the note and he came full of apologies for his earlier intrusion. He was a likeable man, a hard man to refuse.'

On the occasion of his second visit, Eileen had Louise show him directly to her workroom. As he headed towards her, radiating bonhomie, confidence and enthusiasm as well as showing outstretched arms, she moved sideways to avoid that ridiculously insincere two-cheek kissing ritual that was an accepted continental part of social and, now it appeared, business intercourse.

'I knew Monsieur Doucet was grateful I was seeing him. He was quiet, looking around. The place was quivering with samples of materials, drawings and the general clutter of a working artist. I'd purposefully removed the screen and I could almost see him thinking, '*Mon dieu*, she couldn't, she wouldn't have sold it?'

'We settled as you and I are now in front of the fire. That little table there held a tray with a coffee pot, cups, saucers and sugar, as well as a dish of British digestive biscuits. I saw him looking at them. His nostrils widened and I could tell he wasn't impressed.' She gives a small, gleeful laugh.

'I poured, handed him the coffee, hot milk and biscuits, which he refused. I made no attempt at conversation. He sipped at his coffee, reached across for the sugar tongs and clawed out two lumps which he dropped with a plop into his cup. I suspected he was searching for a subject on which to make gracious conversation and would work around to *Le Destin* in due time.'

*

Monsieur Doucet did not disappoint. Leaning back in his chair, he crossed his legs and folded his hands tidily against his stomach. 'Poor Isadora. What a terrible tragedy.'

The talk of Paris that spring was the death of Isadora Duncan's two young children. The dancer was one of the personalities of the era; she had inspired artists to create sculpture, jewelry and paintings of her, and the recently opened Théâtre des Champs-Élysées had her likeness carved in its bas-relief over the entrance. 'Can you imagine the horror of your children dying in a car running backwards into the Seine?'

'Well, no,' said Eileen, 'I can't really.' She may have been waiting for her visitor to start the conversation but she found his subject tedious. The idea of having children had never appealed to her. In fact she found the whole concept of pregnancy and what she presumed had to be the indignity of giving birth to be quite repugnant.

Monsieur Doucet was not put off by her lack of interest. 'She was booked out for her Parisian season, you know. Every ticket sold. But then she is an exquisite dancer. Have you seen her perform?'

'No.'

'Poor little pets and so young. Such a tragedy. And it's even sadder to know that it wouldn't have happened if she weren't such a good mother. She had the chauffeur drive them and their nursemaid to the studio so that, between rehearsals, they could all

44

have lunch together. Deirdre was just seven and Patrick two years younger.' Jacques shook his head. 'I hope their deaths were quick, that they didn't realise what was happening. I'm sure their fathers are distraught.'

'Yes, I'm sure they are.'

Ah, a positive reaction at last, even if it was automatic rather than emphatic. 'Strange, isn't it that Isadora never married? Married to her career, I believe is the modern phrase. And then, imagine, taking two different fathers for her children. A theatre designer and one of the Singers – Paris Singer of the sewing-machine family, you know.'

'Yes, I did know.' Eileen made a poor attempt at stifling a yawn.

'Her behaviour would be socially unacceptable if she wasn't Isadora Duncan but, perhaps, it is understandable being the artist she is. Questionable morals too, you know. And Monsieur Singer was lunching with her and the children that day …'

Monsieur Doucet could no longer avoid picking up on his hostess's lack of interest in the Duncan tragedy, and then he remembered the whispered rumours about Mademoiselle Gray's private life and the company she kept. *Dieu merci*, there was more to Isadora's too. How could he have been so insensitive? He should have stuck to asking Mademoiselle Gray about her various work projects. He retreated to what he hoped would be safer ground by questioning her on how she had come up with the theme, and while she explained about finding the picture in the gallery, he was able to observe her burning dedication.

*

'I never wanted to sell *Le Destin*. I didn't create it to sell.' Miss Gray is at pains to explain to Bruce, to make sure he understands. Her voice in defence is querulously cut glass, still with an edge of Anglo-Irishness. But all these decades later that fact that she did sell her screen resonates with memories that have the power to cause a tightening of her belly.

Bruce is curious. 'So why did you?'

45

She has had a lifetime to mull over that and she still hasn't been able to explain her reason satisfactorily, but she suspects it was to prove as much to herself as to Jacques Doucet that she was a true working woman of the time who, if she so chose, could command above market prices for her work.

Having sidestepped answering Mr Chatwin's question she relents enough to admit, 'I learned my lesson with *Le Destin*, though. I wasn't so quick to let my creations out of my hands again.'

Her fingers worry the indented pattern of her shawl.

Bruce remains quiet. As has already been the case, silence on his part has led to confidences.

'Acquiring *Le Destin* had become an obsession for Jacques Doucet, and it turned out to be the beginning of our working relationship too. Family money allowed him to pursue his passions. He had a great need to surround himself with beauty, and he had a wonderful eye for dressing women; he used beautiful cloth and his trimmings and finish were impeccable. But couture wasn't enough for him.'

Bruce cannot resist asking. 'When *Le Destin* came back on the market this year did you not think of buying it?'

She laughs. It's a harsh, cackling sound. 'What? Buy back my own work? Never. But I am glad Yves Saint-Laurent was such a determined bidder. He has good taste. His clothes are exquisite, and I hear his many homes are opulent without being vulgar.' She makes a little moue, 'It's quite the pity that my screen is going to America.'

Part of her had always regretted not keeping the screen. It had turned out to be her most life-changing piece of work. People may call her E.1027 villa a twentieth-century icon, but it was in the process of creating the screen that, in some subtle way, she had also recreated herself. Somehow the screen enabled her to assume the creative identity that shielded her from the personal loneliness and shyness of her early years.

'When it came to the point did you find it difficult to physically part with *Le Destin*?'

What is with this Mr Chatwin? It is as though he can see into her soul, read her very thoughts and in such an unobtrusive way that one can't take offence. He is leaning towards her, his expression one of sympathetic compassion and his voice gentle and caring.

'Yes.' Why has she admitted to that? She hopes he won't pursue it. Why hadn't she answered him with a blasé 'No', or the Gallic shrug she'd long ago mastered?

'Still, it was the beginning of your international reputation, wasn't it?' He pursues, answering himself. He sounds both in control and optimistic. Yet he is so nice and courteous that she cannot take offence. 'It was all success from then on for you, wasn't it?'

'No. It wasn't. Absolutely not.' Her voice is forceful. Too well, and in too great detail, she remembers what she considers to be her failed projects, the ones that never got beyond drawing, model and planning state. The memory of them still rankles, as does the equally enduring kaleidoscopic pictures of the personal relationships that didn't work out.

She shakes her head backwards and forwards. Her failures and the need to protect her private life are some of the reasons she chooses not to see strangers. Too often these strangers take pleasure in questioning her relentlessly, probing and delving, returning her to places where the pain of disappointment can be such that she no longer wishes to remember. Such as now. Pleasant as Mr Chatwin is, he has succeeded in raking up the embers of her private past.

'Monsieur Doucet asked me to sign *Le Destin*.' She will keep to the subject of her projects.

'And you did sign it, didn't you?' Bruce hopes he is not being too forceful, that she won't insist he leaves, but he wants and needs confirmation from her. Throughout her career, she was known for her refusal to sign her work, and he is curious as to why she had given in on that occasion. He wonders if the rumours about a romantic entanglement between her and Jacques Doucet are true. After all, it is well known that he became her mentor.

'Yes. I wrote my name and the year 1914 on the bottom right-hand corner, and I refused to ever sign anything else.' Her voice is even more forceful but with a touch of what Bruce interprets as false bravado. It is not his wish to upset her – it is not in his character to upset anyone – but he knows enough about human nature and the importance of ensuring the accuracy of a story to know that certain questions must be answered.

Unbelievably he is still here, still accumulating information, hanging by a conversational thread to her company, but how much longer before she asks him to leave? He has another question: 'May I ask, Miss Gray, when and how you first came to Paris?'

She is impressed by the tentative delicacy with which it is asked.

Chapter 7

*I*t was the dawn of the new century and talk of the Boer War dominated London society. Politicians and hostesses alike expressed their
certainty that this 'stubborn breed of Dutch peasants revolting against
the just sovereignty of the Queen,' would soon end in victory, with
Boer republics converted to British colonies. 'The Empire', stated a
newspaper report of the time, 'stretching round the globe, has one
heart, one head, one language, one policy.'

When and how she had first come to Paris? She welcomes Mr
Chatwin's gracefully put question. So graceful that she will answer it
before she sends him away. He deserves an answer.

She clasps her hands. Ah, Paris. The way its scent rose off its
streets to seduce her. The thought of her adopted city still brings a
smile that reaches to the depth of her soul. Within a few hours of
stepping from the train at Gare du Nord and emerging into the street
to the waiting carriage on rue de Maubeuge, she had grown comfortable with its extravagance. Her first impressions remain as powerful
now as they were at the turn of the century. One of the few benefits
of growing old is the way the best of past memories can become
heightened with time.

Thoughts of the wonders of those early days of Paris stop the
clattering images of the scarier childhood intrusions: the solidity
of the Arc de Triomphe's white archway; the fragility of the Eiffel
Tower and the high buildings with their curving wrought iron bal-
conies; the smart, glossy-black, bright-yellow and dark-blue carriages;
horse-drawn omnibuses with the rattle of wheels and the clop, clop of

hooves on the cobbled boulevards; at night the way the street lamps turned the rows of trees into a cabaret of colours, all fairy tresses and brassy crowns, and how the firework displays lit up the skies in great sprays of pink and silver.

She clasps her hands even tighter in memory. 'I first came to Paris in 1900 … such a long time ago.' A little sigh escapes from between her lips. 'It was for one of the great exhibitions of the times – L'Exposition L'Universelle. It was a truly wonderful occasion, one that everyone in London was talking about.'

Earlier in the afternoon, before Mr Chatwin's visit, she had been thinking of her beloved papa, the artist who never achieved the fame he craved, and her favourite brother, Lonsdale, who couldn't wait to go to war. When she thought of one, she thought of the other, the two who had died before their time. Papa painting in Italy – doing what he loved, she supposed, which was some consolation. Lonsdale during the Boer War. Imagine the ridiculousness of a fighting soldier dying from dysentery or enteric, as the death certificate decreed, as a result of bad water. What a waste of a life.

Mama and she had been inconsolable in their grief and they had visited Paris in an effort to break their cycle of sorrow. It hadn't worked for Mama, but the city's ambience had soothed Eileen, wrapped her in its cloak of possibility, seduced her with the dreams of the privacy that could be afforded by living in a foreign city and lured her with its endless creative and social opportunities.

'That exhibition must have been some experience.' Bruce's voice cuts into her reverie.

'It was. Full of the most wonderful sights imaginable.'

Bruce knows about the power of imagination. He too has known wonderful sights – sights that lifted his living from the ordinary to the extraordinary – but while Miss Gray's sights were modern and of the future, his were mostly of the past. He owes that experience to the years he spent working in Sotheby's in London.

He was a reluctant contender for the stylish auction house. After his successful forays on stage at Marlborough College he decided to be an actor, but his father was adamant that no son of his would make a living on the stage, suggesting that, as Bruce had refused to follow him into law, he study architecture.

'That is a ridiculous idea,' Bruce told him, pointing out he hadn't even the basics in maths.

Liking the way the words sounded together, Bruce was going through a phase of defining himself as 'a dodo; illiterate and innumerate'. It didn't stop him harbouring thoughts of going up to Oxford, more for the people he might meet and the reputation of the college than for any degree, although he was wise enough not to admit that to his father.

Having read an article about Sotheby's, his mother, the pacifier in the family, suggested Fine Art as a more suitable career for their son. His father knew somebody who knew someone and, against his will, as he never missed an opportunity of pointing out, in the autumn of 1958 Bruce entered employment at Sotheby's as a numbering porter.

During his first posting he was gauche and uninterested in what he perceived as the menial duties assigned to him; it wasn't until he was transferred to Impressionist sales that he came into his own. 'Imps', as it was known, suited Bruce admirably. It was a glamorous department with a roll call of clients including Hollywood movie stars such as Gregory Peck, David Niven and Elizabeth Taylor. Soon Sotheby's became the main focus of his life.

Under the tutelage of international experts he learned how to describe an object compactly; he had an almost photographic memory and developed what is known in the business as a 'good eye'; he gained a reputation for spotting fakes; he travelled and met a network of rich, aesthetically minded people. His confidence and ability peaked with his elegant cataloguing of a collection of Matisse bronzes.

*

Miss Gray finds she is relaxing into Bruce's likeability. There is something appealing about his beardless, boyish face and gentle but eager manner. She had forgotten how pleasant good company could be. How right he is about the exhibition. 'Some experience,' he'd said.

*

The exhibition opened her eyes to the potential of her future, made her aware of all sorts of possibilities, and it was what she saw there, more than anything else, that blunted the edges of her grief at the deaths of her father and brother and the fact that she no longer lived at Brownswood.

Before coming to Paris, she'd read about L' Exposition and all its innovations in the London *Times,* but, with the surety of youth, she had not quite believed what was written in black and white. Seeing those marvels and more for herself was like stepping into a grown up's fairytale.

Look. Eyes shining, she clasped her hands. She was in Le Grand Palais. There before her was a real model of one of those new flying machines – fragile and delicate as a moth, it captured her attention and spurred her imagination. Having experienced her *baptême de l'air* in England with Charles Rolls who, as well as designing cars, was an ardent balloonist, she loved the sensation of freedom, the surreal feeling of floating above the ground and of viewing the world from aloft. Not only would she fly, she determined, she would learn to fly, become an aviatrix, or a petticoat pilot as the newspapers were calling women who flew.

Times may have been changing, but, ladies of fashion were still encased in heavy corsetry which squeezed their waists into hour-glass shapes, snarled up their insides and were detrimental to their health. From the date of her introduction to a whale-boned corset around the age of eleven, Eileen had sought to circumvent fashion for comfort, and for much of the time she left off the armature of corsetry. She was interested in clothes but favoured the clean lean lines of men's clothing rather than the fripperies that adorned women's outfits of the time: the strangling high-boned collars, hats weighed down with decoration and too-narrow pointed toes of shoes that crippled feet.

But for her visits to the exhibition, to honour and please her mother, she was dressed traditionally and fashionably: a long-skirted suit in that mournful wine colour, Italian kid gloves and her heavy hair piled high under the mandatory wide-brimmed hat, decorated with what she described with a moue as 'half an aviary'. She had that season's fashionable leg o' mutton sleeves, but she'd insisted the seamstress modify their extravagance.

From the time she stepped inside the exhibition hall, clothes and fashion were forgotten. She stood in awe and wonder, unaware of the milling crowds, breathing deeply, enjoying the feeling of the optimism of a new century, the excitement of being at the dawn of the innovations of science and industry. Surrounded by technology and designs of the future, a creeping sense of hope for *her* future was taking over from the grief of loss.

When the monsieur with the sweeping moustache and greasy morning coat, bowing from his waist, assured her that flying was the travel of the future, she had surprised and delighted him by agreeing, and even going as far as confiding to him that she planned to take flying lessons. When he responded too boldly, in a way she considered too familiar, in an instance her stiffening posture, movement of her head and look of hauteur precluded further overtures.

Moving wide-eyed with wonder and enchantment throughout the hall of electric bulbs, all seven thousand twinkling and sparkling at the same time, she felt a little more of the darkness of grieving lift at the implications of permanent light. She had walked away from the hall smiling and, with a sense of purpose, set out to find where the much discussed model of the Chenard-Walker automobile was on view. She had smiled even wider when its impressive reality surpassed her expectations.

She was fascinated by the little she knew about automobiles and interested enough to be able to talk the language of engines and brakes with the young men of her acquaintance. She delighted in borrowing the motors of friends to drive around the streets of London. Picking up a leaflet from the stand she learned that the model on display was designed by Monsieur Chenard. It had a two-cylinder 1160 cc engine which drove the rear wheels through a four-speed gearbox from which there were two drive shafts, one to each rear hub, with the hubs driven by gear teeth cut on the inside.

*

'It was the first time I'd seen cars on show, and it was quite wonderful,' she tells Bruce. These are good memories, memories she is willing to talk about. 'As soon as a model of the Chenard-Walker became available, I resolved to buy one. I placed an order that afternoon, despite the fact that my mother and I were returning to London in a few days.'

'Did you get the car?' Bruce has never heard of a Chenard-Walker, but he'll be able to look it up in the office encyclopaedia.

'I did, but not for a while. Are you interested in cars? The majority of young people today are.'

'Not particularly to drive. But I am interested in their status. While at school I wrote an essay titled "Cars and Characters".'

'And what did you deduce?'

He is intrigued at her interest. In a recollective mode, he locks his hands behind his head and crosses his legs. 'For example, I saw a Rover as exemplifying the solid world of solicitors and accountants; a white Allard showed moral depravity and an addiction to drugs; while a black, midnight-blue or olive-green Rolls Royce gave a clear indication of social respectability – but a red or white one did not.'

She gives a little laugh – well, more of a chuckle. 'I like a sense of humour as much as I like the changing modes of transport. Everyone thought I was joking when a few years ago I expressed an interest in buying a motor scooter, a Vespa – I rather liked their functionality and design. But I was quite serious.'

She is quiet, locked in thought. Perhaps she had always been too serious. Too intent. Of necessity, to survive the pressures of the times, she couldn't be seen as funny and amusing around her mother, who clung to traditional attitudes for her daughters and fought the advances of modernity. With the passage of years she became more decorous, which reflected on Eileen, who ended up as her constant companion. Not that she begrudged the time.

There had been occasions – scarce occasions, but nonetheless, occasions, usually while she was in the throes of a relationship – when she had wanted to be light-hearted and giddy and carefree of all responsibility. They were fleeting moments of utter joy but, always lurking in the background of her mind, she was aware of the social implications for the family if some of her affairs became public knowledge.

'When did you settle in Paris?' Bruce asks. It's a question which he hopes will keep open their lines of communication.

'It took a few years before I was able to move permanently here. At that time my mother and I were living in South Kensington.'

'But I thought you lived in Ireland?'

'Oh, yes, we did, just outside the town of Enniscorthy. That's where our home, Brownswood, was.'

'Was?'

'Yes, was.' She crimps closed her lips. The subject is not for pursuing.

Bruce knows all about the upheaval of moving house. During his early childhood, while his father was away at the war, every-one he knew seemed to be on the move, renting out their houses, having guests to stay, trying to second guess and avoid enemy bombardments. His mother shuttled him back and forth on the railways of wartime England, between Filey and a dozen addresses in Birmingham, Stratford, Baslow, Dronfield, Buxton and Leamington Spa. He had loved the sounds of those words and the adventures they implied.

He remembers as vividly as a Pathé news sequence the times they moved, escorted by the drone of airplanes, bright searchlights and shrill sirens. The gusting steam from the giant engine of the train, always, it seemed, waiting for them at a fogbound station, followed by the clunk of closing carriage doors. The carriage seats were hard, the cigarette smoke suffocating and the sounds from the mouth-organs dirge-like. Due to his early years of living out of suitcases and sleeping in strange beds in even stranger bedrooms, Bruce believes he has acquired an inbuilt restlessness and the need to be constantly moving.

He won't mention any of this to Miss Gray. He has never been inclined to divulge information about himself. As long as he is listening and commenting impersonally and objectively, he can hide inside his own yarns. He notices things, the smallest of details, and in noticing he invents; hovering between fact and fiction he enters the intimacy of people's lives without them knowing, with the result that he has a fund of stories about people he has met and situations he has found himself in. Some of his stories are based on fact, others a mix of fact and fiction and more are pure fiction.

Now that she has answered his question about her first impressions of Paris, he feels he can ask: 'Why did you move to London?'

Chapter 8

*T*he move to London had started a long time before Eileen and her mother actually packed up their possessions and organised permanent residency at the family's townhouse in Kensington. On previous occasions The Boltons was only opened for the Season or to attend the Royal Meeting at Ascot. Now it was to be their home. For always and ever.

As far as Eileen was concerned, the change in her family's life began on one of those days when she was doing something 'forbidden' again. If her grandfather found out, he would chuck her under her chin and tell her she must learn to obey her 'elders and betters'. If she wasn't doing something that Lizzie considered dangerous, she might give her a hug to encourage her to 'spread her little wings'. She could never be sure what her mama would do. Perhaps slap her palms with her ruler – two slaps on each hand; smile vaguely, as though she hadn't absorbed her daughter's naughtiness; or quietly admonish – 'Really, dear, you shouldn't, you mustn't' – before returning to either her embroidery or letter-writing.

Eileen's forbidden had not only brought her hopping, skipping and jumping the whole way down the avenue. Forbidden also had her sticking her head between the thick bars of the gate so that she could look out to the wide world that lay beyond the boundary of Brownswood.

It was April, nearly the feast of Easter. Late afternoon sunshine cast long shadows from the trees and hedges that bordered the dirt track leading up the hillside to their house. Through the gaps in the greenery she could see into the sweep of meadows, in shades of the palest green and lemony gold, and watch the newborn lambs wobbling on shaky legs. The sky was powder blue and full of fluffy clouds, the way she loved it.

When she heard the sounds of a carriage, wiggling her shoulders, she reached out her neck as far through the bars as it would go. A visitor would be an unexpected excitement. Most of the people who journeyed this far from the town were coming to call on her family, as there was little else beyond their estate. After a final stretch of her neck she was rewarded by the sight of the carriage from the railway station, with Old Billy sitting atop waving his whip. When he saw her, he removed his hat and with an exaggerated flourish swept it across his body in a bow.

'Wait till you see who I've got in the back,' he shouted, swinging the horse around to draw to a halt outside the gates. When Papa stepped out of the carriage Eileen thought her heart would burst. In her excitement to greet him the ribbon in her hair snagged on the bars and her smock tore on a spike. None of that mattered. When Billy pulled open the gates, she jumped into Papa's arms and rode up the avenue sitting on his knees, encircled within his arms, his cheek resting against her head.

Eileen was the youngest and most beloved of James Maclaren Smith's children. She was conceived during a night of passion on his return from a painting expedition in Italy. She was a child of moods and emotions, never finding but constantly looking for what she called 'the happiness fairies'. When anyone bothered enough to take the time to ask what she meant, she'd explain with the solemnity of certainty that her happiness fairies were like Lizzie's saints, the ones who wore haloes of goodness above their heads.

She was first out of the carriage, and she ran shouting all the way around to the back of the house – the front door was only ever used when visitors were expected or when Papa was at home – 'Papa's back, Papa's back. Mama, do you hear? Grandfather, where are you?'

Lizzie stuck her head out of the kitchen and called on her to shush, saying that she was making enough noise to wake the dead. By the time Eileen had reached the hallway, her sisters Ethel and Thora were looking over the banisters, refusing to be excited. Much of their time was spent practising 'being ladylike'. Mama, still holding her pen, came out from the drawing room where she had been sitting at her bureau writing more letters.

'Papa's home.' Eileen jigged up and down.

'What are you talking about? Where is he?'

Eileen could see Mama's excitement in the widening of her eyes and the way her pale hand fluttered to her neck. And then Papa was there, so big and handsome, blocking the sunlight from the little window. He was smiling and holding his arms wide as he came up the steps from the scullery to the hall.

'Really, James,' said Mama, still standing at the threshold to the drawing room. 'You might at least have waited until we opened the hall door for you.'

'Ah, but I couldn't delay that long.' And there in front of everyone, even Lizzie, her papa lifted her mama off the ground and swirled her around and around, his feet dancing on the black and white tiles. And Mama was laughing and blushing as Papa was whispering into her hair.

Billy came up the backstairs with the portmanteau holding Papa's clothes. By the time he started carrying in rolls of canvases and stacks of paintings, a few completed but the majority incomplete, Papa and Mama, arms wrapped around each other, had gone upstairs. The excitement grew mighty as Billy continued to carry in Papa's stuff: his Gladstone bag – which Eileen knew would be full of half-squeezed tubes of paint, wondrous colours with wondrous names like vermillion, her favourite cobalt blue and yellow ochre – as well as a big bundle of brushes and all sorts of boxes and parcels haphazardly tied with string and ribbons.

Lizzie, tucking her flyaway hair behind her ears and smoothing her apron across her belly, took control. She organised the lighting of the fire in the drawing room; arranged for vases of fresh daffodils to be placed on the side tables; opened up the piano, dusted the keys and oversaw the baking of Irish soda bread. For supper they'd have mutton broth and a boiled chicken which Paddy would have to kill immediately. Where was her husband? He was never around when he was needed. Oh, and they'd better wash the blue willow-patterned dishes the master liked. 'He will enjoy his supper, though it won't be food the mistress will have on her mind,' she said, hands on hips and with a knowing look upwards.

Later that evening, when the gas lamps were lit and the turf fire was scenting the drawing room, Mama called Eileen. Her sisters and brothers had already been summoned and dismissed. They had talked to Papa of their recent academic achievements, not that either they or Papa were particularly interested in schooling, but Mama insisted they report to their father. It was only after they had 'comported' – Mama's favourite word about her children's behaviour – to her satisfaction did she allow them to receive their presents; she could be relied on to spoil every occasion, even a little bit. When he was happy, Papa was happy without reservation. That was one of the things everyone loved about him.

When Eileen entered the room, Papa, his legs spread wide, was standing by the fire smoking a cigar. Through the blackness of the windows, Eileen saw the moon rising, turning from a pale pinky orange to a buttery gold. Everything about Brownswood was different when her father was home. She was too young then to identify the reasons, although some years later she realised the change in the atmosphere of the house was due to the sense of energy that surrounded Papa and the air of happiness he wore like a velvet cloak.

Several of the boxes Billy had carried in were stacked up on the floor. From them spilled lengths of silks in hot bright-pinks, blues and yellows; some bonnets with swooping and curling ostrich feathers of the most tickly, softest variety; yards of decorative braids studded with gold; and the daintiest of suede gloves in pale grey and cream with the tiniest of pearl buttons.

Eileen's eyes were drawn to the sofa: perched on its back was the most beautiful doll she had ever seen. She was pale skinned with tumbling golden curls, unblinking green eyes, a rosebud mouth and pale raggedy limbs. Eileen thought she would die of happiness when Papa handed it to her.

'Is this for me?' She was not used to receiving presents. Her few toys had belonged to her brothers and sisters, and her clothes were mostly pass-me-downs.

'Yes, my pet. It's yours. I chose it especially for you.'

'Is it mine? Really mine?' she asked.

Mama came over and wrapped her arms around Papa. She told Eileen to give him a thank-you kiss and that it was time for her to go to bed.

'Can I bring her?' Eileen asked.

'Of course you may, my pet,' he said softly. 'And you must think of a name for her.'

'Will you help?'

Her father looked at her mother, who frowned, and then he said, 'No, you must do that. She's yours. Choose whatever name you wish.'

'I will, oh, I will.' She could think no further than the joy of ownership. Her very own doll. She could not remember owning a real anything all of her own before. That was because she was an 'after-thought', she'd heard Lizzie tell Paddy.

As Eileen carried the doll carefully up the stairs, the moon flooded the grounds of Brownswood with light while the sky deepened from smoky blue to a deep sapphire that was almost navy. She was engulfed with waves of happiness. When she reached her small room, tucked into the attic, she laid Doll on her bed and carefully spread out the pink satin of her gown.

Over the next weeks Brownswood pulsated with life. All sorts of people, from the vicar and the priest to the schoolmaster, the doctor and the local constable, visited to leave their cards or just called in to say hello and welcome back the master. There were formal parties of elegant men and women, as well as artists, musicians and poets. They sat around the large mahogany dining table eating the finest of food off the Pounden family's precious Spode dinner service and drinking the best of wines from Grandpa's cellar, served in Waterford crystal glasses. Invariably those dinners evolved into musical evenings, when the notes from the piano, violins and accordions had the household tapping and humming.

In between the parties and the fun there were the usual raised voices. For as long as Eileen could remember, that was the way it was with Mama and Papa. Quite horrid. On his return from his painting trips, indoor harmony lasted only for a short while. It was followed by shouting and rows and lots of banged doors and then he went off again on his travels. Each time he left, the soul of Brownswood went with him. Eileen and her brothers and sisters had grown up used to the see-sawing times of happiness followed by loneliness, to the house full of guests and a table groaning with plenty, to empty rooms giving way to an air of gloom and beastly food.

This time, Eileen thought, the voices of her parents seemed louder than previously, and she was sure the door banging was more frequent. She used to sit on the floor outside the door of her mother's bedroom, rocking backwards and forwards, holding Doll in her arms, thinking if she wished hard enough her papa and mama would stop shouting at each other. But they didn't. When her father shouted, his voice deep and thundering, she hid her face in Doll's golden hair. When Mama raised her voice, she held Doll close to her, like a shield, and thought of how much she hated Spode dishes. 'Fiddly curlicues and silly flowers', was how Papa described them, throwing his hands in the air and rolling his eyes in a way that made her laugh.

Young as she was, Eileen was aware that the problem between her parents lay with the Poundens, which was the name of Mama's family. Mama had returned from Europe to Brownswood, to Grandma and Grandpa, bringing her husband and four children, when she'd tired of the nomadic, hand-to-mouth existence as the wife of a wandering artist. Eileen learned this from listening to Lizzie and whoever happened to be visiting her in the kitchen. They'd sit on either side of the big table gossiping among themselves, as though she wasn't there. And invariably she was, perched on the trestle bed, enjoying the warmth from the range and the cosiness of chat. Lizzie and her visitors talked about everything from the difficulties with the potato crop to the problems of selling the strawberries from the gardens of Brownswood in Dublin, from the hardships of the Famine to the wandering souls of November, and eventually most talk would lead to her mama's elopement.

Elopement?

She had asked Lizzie what that meant. When Lizzie explained, Eileen knew the shouting couldn't matter too much when her mama loved her papa so much that she'd run off with him to get married, although Lizzie explained how she'd come back before Eileen was born. Eileen knew she could never love anyone enough to run away from Brownswood. Papa did not appear to have any relatives, but Mama made up for his lack. The Pounden family was powerful and important around the town of Enniscorthy, and indeed throughout the county of Wexford, as well as in the cities of Dublin and London, and not forgetting Scotland.

Mama made sure her children were imbued with their heritage. She would sit on the low chair with the tapestry seat, her pale, slender hands with their perfectly oval-ed nails idling over her latest piece of embroidery, while they sat on the floor in a circle around her.

Painstakingly she explained how her mother – their grandmother – was Lady Jane Stuart, daughter of Francis Stuart, 10th Earl of Moray. 'Where is Moray?' she'd ask at that point in her discourse. And they'd all wave their arms and shout, 'Scotland!'

Their grandmother's first husband was Sir John Archibald Drummond Stewart, 6th Baronet Stewart of Grandtully, who died in May 1838, and in August of the same year she had married Jeremiah Lonsdale Pounden. Mama, born three years later, was their only child. She'd finish her recital with a deep sigh which embraced the fragile positions of privilege and power. 'And as such I held the future of the family in my hands, and still do.' She left her five children in no doubt that they had inherited the reins of family protection and responsibility. They, after all, were her successors.

The position of successor was one which Eileen preferred not to think about, as that would mean Mama was dead. When timidly she'd voiced her fears to Lizzie about the worry of being a successor, Lizzie gave her a jokey little push and said with a funny laugh, 'It's only Master James who has to worry about that. And may God help us all when he marries.'

*

Across from Miss Gray, Bruce sits immobile, his hands resting on his lap, his expression alive with interest. He is lost in her story, listening and absorbing, visualising Brownswood, creating settings and dialogue with a young Eileen to the fore, her parents, siblings and all-pervading Lizzie to the background. He has forgotten that he should be assembling information for an interview, forgotten the implications of returning empty-handed to Mr Linklater, forgotten about the unopened moleskine notebook in his pocket.

From Miss Gray's point of view, Mr Chatwin's presence is unobtrusive. There is no harm in remembering, and it is pleasant to have a young gentleman sitting opposite while one does.

*

Papa was bending over her.

'Shush.' He put his fingers to her lips. 'Don't make a sound.'

Eileen sat up. He was wearing his travelling cloak and carrying his small leather portmanteau. She could smell his cologne and in the dimness of the dawn light see the silvery bits of his hair curling at the back of his collar.

She sat bolt upright, the veins in her neck pounding.

'Where are you going?'

'Shush. Back to Italy.'

'You can't. Don't go, Papa. Please. Please.' She held out her arms and he sat heavily on the bed beside her, which made the springs ping and creak.

'I have to.'

'Then take me with you.' She scrabbled under the quilt for Doll. She could be ready in a few minutes. She knew about travel. The family had been to the continent on several occasions.

'I can't.' He straightened up. 'Remember, you're my special pet. No scenes. Don't make an awkward situation more difficult than it already is,' he whispered. He was treating her as though she were an adult. It gave her hope.

'I just want to be with you,' she whispered back.

'And I want you with me, too. But in this life, we can't always have what we want.'

'You and Mama were fighting again,' she accused. 'I heard you.' She hoped her father would reassure her that this was not so.

Papa didn't like unpleasantness or the thought of anyone being upset. When conflict had to be faced, he frequently gentled it. 'Not really fighting,' he said. 'It was more of a disagreement. Your mother and I think differently on various subjects.'

'It was a shouting disagreement.'

He sighed. 'I suppose you could say that. Perhaps I did raise my voice a wee bit.'

Eileen relaxed a little. It was good to have her father's exclusive attention. 'I heard Mama shouting, not you,' she fibbed and felt awful once the lie was out of her mouth.

'Ladies don't shout. And your mama's a lady. A great lady. Always remember that.'

Eileen would do anything to keep her father with her. 'But you're not a gentleman.' It was a statement more than a query.

'No, I'm not,' he agreed. He laid his mouth close to her ear. 'It'll be our secret. If you don't, I'll never tell anyone that I'm not a gentleman.'

'Mama knows,' Eileen whispered back.

'Are you certain?'

'Yes. I heard her tell Ethel. She said, "Your father's no gentleman." That means you, doesn't it?'

''Fraid so. And remember, your mama's always right. And now, my pet ...'

'No, Papa. Please. No. You can't go.'

'I have to.'

There was a rushing static around her. It sealed her off so completely from him and the room and everything she was familiar with that his voice seemed to reach her from afar. It was as though he had already left.

'When will you be back?'

As he stood up, he bent down and smoothed the quilt, spreading it evenly over her with the palm of his hand, before leaning towards her to brush her cheek with his lips. She jerked backwards. If he was going to leave her, she would not allow him to kiss her, nor would she kiss him.

He stood up, straightened his shoulders and looked down at his daughter. She was raised on an elbow, the soft cambric of her night-gown touching her neck; her cheeks were rosy with sleep and her chestnut hair curled around her face. His sleepy angel. He picked up his portmanteau and left.

When he was gone from the room, Eileen listened to the heavy sound of his footsteps along the corridor; she imagined him going down the stairs, creaking on the last step, walking through the hall and out the front door. Only then did she climb out of bed and stand by the window. The dogcart was drawn up at the bottom of the front steps with Paddy holding the reins.

Her papa, tall and handsome, came down the stone steps and moved away from the house so that he could look up at the bedroom windows and higher into the attic. But Eileen shifted back into the shadows. She balled her hands into such tight fists that she could feel her fingernails digging into her palms. She concentrated on the pain of marking her skin. As she looked out at the hedges sheathed in morn-ing mist, she couldn't be sure that the mist wasn't her tears. When she relaxed her hands, there was a row of sharp, sore marks across her palm.

She did not care that Papa was gone again; she wouldn't cry. She had Brownswood. It was her home and it couldn't get up and go away. She knew every nook and cranny of the place – inside and outside – and she loved its aura of familiar comfort, reinforced by the shabby gentility of worn carpets, mismatched furniture, sun-streaked velvet curtains and faded wallpaper.

Brownswood's land stretched further than her eyes could see. Even when she was not allowed outside, she was able to escape confinement by looking out the window at the thread of the river Slaney, wandering like a blue and silver ribbon, curling and looping through the fields of black and white cattle. The longer she stood quietly and intently, the larger and more extravagantly remote landscape and sky became.

James Maclaren Smith did not look back as he was driven away, but Eileen peeped out of the window until the carriage was hidden by the curve of the avenue. He always came home.

Chapter 9

*L*izzie, sleeves rolled up and plump, dimpled arms wobbling up and down, was beating sugar into butter, walloping the mixture up the sides of the bowl with her big wooden spoon. With a heavy sigh, she straightened her back and ran a limp hand across her red cheeks. These days, she did a lot of sighing.

Eileen was sitting on the trestle in the corner of the kitchen cuddling Doll while rocking backwards and forwards, holding her loneliness for her papa like a plum in her mouth and hoping for a lick of cake mixture.

'When do you think my papa will be back?'

Lizzie gave a distracted click of her tongue. 'Now, don't you be going on with your questions and your poor mother just a shadow of her self.' With another great sigh, she began cracking eggs into the mixture.

Eileen knew Mama was upset but she didn't know why. She didn't think she'd misbehaved. She cast back her mind over the previous weeks but couldn't remember doing anything that would account for her mother being shadowy. She was behaving in a different way than usual and Eileen found it scary. Everyone noticed the way she was carrying on, as Lizzie would say, but nobody did anything about it.

Mama had stopped doing embroidery and was no longer writing letters. Whatever about the embroidery, she was always writing letters and little notes and thank-yous and how-are-yous. But now, when she wasn't nursing the vapours lying on her bed with the curtains drawn so tightly across the windows that the sunshine was blocked out, she was walking around the house wearing an old wrapper, her hair trailing down her back, twisting at her handkerchief. Sometimes Lizzie followed as she went from room to room and back again, touching a framed photograph here, plumping up a cushion there, snapping at anyone who crossed her path, her eyes red and sad.

'Sit down for a minute and take the weight off your feet,' Lizzie would say, concern stamped on her kindly features.

But Mama just kept on at whatever she was doing; it was as though she couldn't be bothered hearing.

'Why is she like this?' Eileen would ask. As she had nothing else to do, she spent much of her time trailing after Mama and Lizzie, clutching Doll.

'Ah sure, Lord help us, it runs in the family, and she can't help herself,' Lizzie would answer with a sad little shake of her head.

'What's in the family? How can something run in the family?' Eileen wanted to know.

'Nothing. It's not your concern for now. God help us. It's time enough for you to know when you have to.' Lizzie clamped shut her lips with a little click.

When Eileen asked Ethel what Lizzie meant about the thing that was making Mama funny 'running in the family', her sister caught her by the arm and pinched it so hard that Eileen gasped. 'Don't you ever say anything like that ever again. Do you hear me? Never. To anyone. Ever.' As an added deterrent, she shook Eileen so roughly that her head bounced backwards and forwards and her teeth chattered.

That summer Ethel and Thora were too busy being themselves to bother with anyone else, much less a 'mad mother' and a 'silly sister', as they said, giggling from behind their hands while darting from room to room. The talk among the few visitors who came to Brownswood was of Queen Victoria's Golden Jubilee celebrations. Ethel and Thora hung on every word about the queen, the court diary and the princes and princesses. They said they were 'seeking to reinvigorate their social lives' – not that Eileen knew what that meant. But, as tennis parties, going riding, visiting Dublin, attending balls and bullying Mama to allow them to spend time in London was how they occupied themselves, she thought that's what 'reinvigoration' must involve. Even when she was as old as them, she wouldn't be bothered with reinvigoration.

Her brothers weren't around either. She missed the dashing red of Lonsdale's Dragoon Guards uniform, but from overheard conversations she learned he was too busy being a soldier to bother with Brownswood and family. James, who had graduated from Cambridge University with a Master of Arts, appeared to be equally busy with the 5th Battalion Rifle Brigade.

Lizzie straightened up again and began scooping flour into the bowl. 'The mistress will never get used to it,' she said.

'Used to what?' asked Paddy, who'd come in from the yard hoping for a mug of tea. He was a kind man with a sad face.

'The master being gone for good, of course.'

Lizzie's concentration was complete as she added a stream of porter to the cake mixture. Eileen wondered if she'd heard right: her father always came home.

'Papa will be coming back, won't he?' Her smoky eyes were huge in her troubled face. Clasping Doll tightly to her chest, she came to stand square in front of Lizzie, who, with tongue tipping out the side of her mouth in concentration, was adding currants, raisins and sultanas to the cake mixture.

She looked up from stirring, the wooden spoon dripping dark globules of floury porter. 'No, *macushla*, he won't. Not this time.' Her voice was softened: she knew how fond the little one was of the master – like his shadow, she was. Poor child – it was little enough attention she got from the rest of the family. And for once she wasn't bothering her to lick the spoon. Contrary as Paddy was with wanting those endless mugs of tea, she'd miss him if he took off. Head down, she bent back to the cake mixture in her yellow and white bowl.

Eileen stood for a moment, absorbing the enormity of what she'd just heard. Gulping for air, she ran from the kitchen, thumping along the hallway and up the stairs. Papa never coming back: it wasn't possible. And nobody had told her. She stood on the half landing, letting the beams of yellow sunshine wash over her. Chin jutting, she was as still as a statue while she felt the iciness of cold break out all over her body. It came in stabs of shivers. When she looked down her hands were shaking. They didn't look as though they belonged to her at all.

In a sudden, violent movement, she held up Doll. Eyes narrowing, she looked at it as though she had never seen it before. Grasping it by its soft shoulders, she shook and shook until its hair flayed backwards and forwards and its limbs shot out in all directions. Swinging it by one arm, she entered her mother's room where she opened cupboards and rummaged through drawers, her small fingers flying through the contents and her heart palpitating. Finally she found what she was looking for in the needlework box beside the frame which held a tightly stretched linen afternoon-tea cloth. It wasn't finished, although its border of purple pansy flowers had been nearly completed before Papa had come home. Mama loved pansies. Pansies for remembrance, she said.

Dangling Doll by its hair, Eileen ran back to her room, threw it on her bed and straddled it. Only then did she examine the silvery, pointed scissors she'd taken from Mama's room.

With her knees pressing deep into the patchwork quilt, she chopped off Doll's hair, beginning with the curls falling down over its shoulders and finishing when the crown was nothing more than short stubble. All the while Doll looked back at her out of those unblinking green eyes, its rosebud mouth uncomplaining and the sweetness of its expression unsullied as Eileen stabbed and stabbed at it with the sharp points of the scissors. She slashed through the bodice of its satin gown until the material was flittered and crumbs of sawdust from Doll's insides spilled out over the bed.

*

James Maclaren Smith's timing of leaving his family could not have been worse. He had left two daughters and two sons of marriageable age. Society, which favoured the Pounden family, was quick to pass judgement on him, sniffing that as he had not been reared to service and duty he was unlikely to be the type of man to be preoccupied by the social consequences of his actions.

During the rein of Queen Victoria, coming from a broken family did not bode well for sons or daughters of nobility wishing to make good marriages. Despite the queen's own penchant for sketching and collecting drawings of male nude figures, she claimed to have the highest of morals, and she let it be known that she expected the same from her subjects. Outwardly, at least, she was given it. Divorced women were not received at court. In the broader social circles of the time, a husband leaving his wife cast aspersions on that wife, even when the husband was regarded as feckless and socially inferior. No smoke without fire, it was said.

In the beginning, when the subject of Ethel's betrothal to Englishman Henry Tufnell Campbell was broached, Mama was wary about the match. She worried at the unlikelihood of it being realised and fretted at the slighting of the Pounden family if the Campbells decided such a match was inappropriate.

After all, Henry was not merely an only son: he was the only child of Lady Anne Katherine Bethune, daughter of Sir Henry Bethune of Kilconquhar, 1st Bt. and Coutts Trotter, and John Thomas Campbell. The idea of her eldest daughter making such an alliance delighted and terrified Mama in equal measure. In the circumstances, as a woman abandoned by her husband, it was almost too good to be true and would be regarded even in the drawing rooms of socially aware, fashionable London as prestigious.

When the announcement of the betrothal was made, and with the wedding plans proceeding smoothly, Mama began to recover her spirits, embrace her social duties and bask on the laurels of social approbation.

'Quite like her old self, isn't she?' Lizzie gushed plump approval with nods and smiles. She was the latest of her family to serve at Brownswood. For as far back as anyone could remember it had been her ancestors' lot to see to the comfort and care of the Pounden family. Finally her mistress was coming into her own, and about time too. For the first time in her life, her mistress was on her own and solely responsible for her actions: her mother had died in 1880 and her father seven years later, the year before Ethel's wedding.

The mistress had been shaken out of mourning her beloved father by the necessity of organising pre-wedding tea parties, tennis afternoons and punting picnics by the river. Her time was occupied poring over samples of silks, velvets and brocades from Dublin, London and Paris. She ordered the best quality in the most fashionable shades and called in the local seamstress.

It was years before Eileen saw the situation clearly enough to realise that once the wedding became a likelihood her mother would have done anything – well, almost anything – to ensure that Ethel married Henry Tufnell Campbell. The wedding would ensure the continuance of the Poundens' social status.

Young as she was then, Eileen still has full recall of the sensation of uneasiness clawing and gnawing in the pit of her belly, how uncomfortable and ridiculous she felt hovering on the brink of the elaborate wedding preparations. Everything changed, became too elaborate, and the comings and goings of the people who visited weren't fun, not like when Papa was around.

When she closed her eyes at night, in the darkness she could see plates of daintily arranged triangles of cucumber, ham and chicken sandwiches sprinkled with watercress; tiered cake stands accommodating neat wedges of Victoria sponge, slim fingers of buttery shortbread and moist slivers of porter cake. The food and beverages were consumed with more politeness than enjoyment by the guests who called in their uninvited droves.

Eileen hated the false jollity and insincerity of the socialising surrounding the wedding. She particularly disliked the simpering prinking of the matrons and daughters, hanging hopefully on the edge of an introduction to one of Henry's 'so appropriate' friends. She heard a Mrs Jones say, 'You couldn't be sure but an introduction might, just might, lead to a suitable marriage.'

With the jaundiced eye of a child, she decided if marrying meant going through all that palaver, she would 'pass' – as she had heard the ladies at Mama's card parties say. She would be quite happy living out her life at Brownswood, and that's what she planned to do.

*

'Do you return often to Ireland?'

The timing of Bruce Chatwin's question is impeccable. For a moment Eileen Gray is still the young girl in the laced boots and sashed dress, absorbed in the unfolding drama of Ethel's wedding. Then the old woman, with so little loving and so much losing in her life, is brought back to the present.

'No, I don't go back to Ireland. Not any more.'

He is somewhat taken aback, as he has developed an impression from Miss Gray that her home, Brownswood, in the widest sense of sanctuary, was important to her.

'Although I did return in 1929 for the sale of the house and lands,' she says, her voice fading into space.

Her expedition was against the advice of everyone and her reasons for returning were personal. By doing so she hoped to recapture the peace and innocence of her childhood and lay to rest the ghosts of her memories. But it hadn't happened like that: while everything and yet nothing had changed, the veil was cruelly torn from the recollections she had so carefully cherished. If anything, her memories were too sharpened with negatives which, knife-like, cut into her; the grief she had felt as a child was intensified into an aching maturity.

Brownswood and its twenty-four acres of land were bought by the Wexford Health Board for £5,000, its destiny to serve as the county sanatorium for patients with the disease of consumption that was rife in Ireland.

As she was driven away from her home for the last time, she had looked out the back window of the motorcar at the forlorn building, unkempt grounds overrun with weeds and meadows empty of cattle.

'Going back was a mistake,' she says. 'I should have left the sale in the hands of the agent.'

Bruce is skilled at sensing the moods of people. He is back in interview mode: finding and using parallels and chimings between Miss Gray and her stories. Despite her colourful life and undoubted success, he hasn't changed his opinion: Miss Gray's chime is one of vulnerability.

'Didn't you miss Brownswood?' he asks tentatively.

Her reply is more heartfelt than ever she intended. 'Oh, I did, I do miss Brownswood, so very much. I always have. Probably always will.

It was home.' Caught unexpectedly by the question, her lips pucker and her eyes blink; she pokes under the sleeve of her grey cardigan, extracts a small, rather grubby lace-trimmed handkerchief and blows her nose.

It's heartbreaking to see.

With a flash of shame at his teenage arrogance Bruce remembers insisting, rather dramatically, when he was old enough to have read Baudelaire, that he developed 'a case of *la grande maladie: horreur de domicile*', which was merely another of the dramatic stories he fabricated about himself, as were his blasé remarks about Birmingham being no more than a place to leave. But despite his dramatic shrugs of dismissal, Brown's Green Farm was home and it provided an ongoing cushion of security. And he couldn't imagine the way his life would be if his home hadn't existed

Making a conscious effort at exerting control, Miss Gray replaces the handkerchief, raises her head and sits a little straighter. 'When my sister married, her husband decided he wanted them to live in Brownswood. My mother was delighted at the thought of having a man around the house and children filling the corners with laughter. She and my sisters were very close.'

She doesn't want to be disloyal to the memory of her family, particularly her mother, by talking of the betrayal. Hadn't she learned to exercise discretion and chosen to live much of her personal life in shadows, careful to avoid the slightest whiff of a scandal getting back to the family?

'And after their wedding your sister and her husband came to live at Brownswood?' The question is a gentle probe that brings with it a rush of memories that Eileen Gray tries to push aside.

Wasn't it Sigmund Freud who advocated theories of the unconscious mind and repression? And who pioneered the practice of psychoanalysis through dialogue between doctor and patient – the Talking Cure, as it became known. How many late-night, smoke-filled, absinthe-fuelled discussions had that same talking cure provoked during the 1920s?

What has led her to think of Freud now?

Because, even after all this time, her childhood memories of leaving Brownswood are painful and her feelings of hurt and betrayal are as powerful as ever. Had she expected them to be different?

She became obsessed with stories of Famine evictions, likening them to what she called her 'eviction' from Brownswood. Mama smacked her on her hand and told her not to be so ridiculous. The hurt of leaving her home was physical as well as psychological: knots in her belly, tightness in her middle, shivers of fear running up and down her spine and that all-enveloping sensation of futility and sadness that at the time she was too young to identify but that never left her.

Throughout the journey by carriage to the railway station at Enniscorthy, the train to Dublin city, by carriage again to Kingstown, express steamer from Kingstown Harbour to the port of Holyhead in Wales and the final journey by railway, Mama had kept talking brightly about living in London.

'Yes, my sister and her husband had decided to make their home at Brownswood.'

'Did you like him – this Mr Tufnell?' Bruce's query returns her to the present. His voice is soft and soothing, as though he is talking to a child.

Miss Gray doesn't reply immediately. She has never had to answer that question, never been asked it. She shifts on the cushion of her chair, her feet moving the cat who stirs slightly before settling back, with a few purrs, on her shoes. Time has stolen the flesh from her buttocks. No matter how plump the cushion, she becomes stiff and uncomfortable when she sits in one place for too long.

Chapter 10

*T*hroughout her life Miss Gray has tried to avoid dwelling on the subject of Henry Tufnell Campbell. She has always pushed him determinedly to the back of her mind. Successful as she has been at excising thoughts of the man – well, most of the time – she has never forgotten her first sight of him. Like Bruce Chatwin, she has found first impressions to be invariably accurate. And Henry Tufnell Campbell, she was quick to decide, was quite horrid.

As he stood in the hallway of Brownswood, holding his top hat by its brim in front of his belly, she hadn't known who this strange man was or why he was visiting. After a quick look, she decided whoever he was she didn't like him.

Watching from her perch on the stairs, her knuckles grew white with intensity as her hands grasped at the banisters, and when she poked out her head between the slats, the sash of her dress caught in her heel (her clothes were constantly torn – she said it wasn't her fault or she couldn't help it, but such explanations didn't prevent her getting a clip around the ear from Lizzie or a smack on her hands from Mama). She ignored the ripping sound as, fascinated and repulsed, she watched the stranger's antics.

Imagine! He went so close to the gilt-framed mirror that his nose seemed to be touching it. Then he opened his mouth. While moving his head backwards and forwards, he appeared to be examining his teeth. After which he stuck out his tongue. Eileen was sure it was as far down his chin as it would go – certainly it was further than she was able to get hers. She knew that because she'd been intrigued enough to copy his gestures. Finally, he licked his finger – the long one beside his thumb – and ran it along his moustache. She had never seen a grown-up behave in such a way.

From Lizzie's fussing in the kitchen, Eileen knew Ethel was due to return home from visiting friends in Wicklow that afternoon. She'd come back about half an hour ago, all flustered, and ran up the stairs to her bedroom. Eileen hadn't known a man would be calling. So he had to be the reason Mama had insisted she wear her best and newest dress. Worst of all, last night she'd got Lizzie to squeeze Eileen's hair into tightly knotted rags until her head was so scrunched in misery that she feared her hair would fall out. In the morning the scrunches had transformed into these horrid ringlets and left her with an aching head. All that going on wouldn't be for Ethel's benefit alone.

Who was he? Where were Ethel and Thora? There was no sign of Mama either, and her presence these days was everywhere. How long was this stranger going to remain standing there?

When Ethel appeared down the stairs, brushing past Eileen as though she wasn't there, she was smiling, patting her hair into place and wearing her new gown. Eileen had watched each stage of its creation with curiosity – from the choosing of the material to the style, fittings and trimmings. It was the latest fashion. Eileen knew its attributes by heart. The style and making up of clothes, as well as material and colour, were the parts she found interesting – *not* having to wear them.

The design for Ethel's gown was taken from a picture in a magazine all the way from Paris. The gown was made from corded silk in a heliotrope shade, decorated with *passementèrie*, with sleeves gathered at the shoulders and fastened at the wrist with a row of small black buttons. From the look of it, and the narrowness of its waist, Eileen knew it had to be just as uncomfortable – if not even more so – than Ethel's and Thora's other gowns. She was used to seeing her sisters holding in their breaths, hanging onto the bedpost while being laced into their stays, either by each other or by Lizzie. She was determined she would never be so squeezed, even when she had grown up to be a lady.

During the past weeks of feverish wedding organisation, Eileen had served her own penance of standing still for fittings and being pricked with pins. All for this pink frock which Mama had insisted she wear this afternoon. She looked down at its frills and ribbons and looked back to the man in the hallway, still clutching his hat. His presence must be something to do with Ethel's wedding, she decided. These days everything that happened in Brownswood was.

Watching him, she was struck by a horrid thought. He couldn't be the person Ethel was going to marry? Who would be her brother-in-law? Surely not? Brother-in-law Henry – she ran the phrase around her mouth and looked again – Ethel couldn't be marrying that man.

Eileen sat on the stairs, rigid with the awfulness of the knowledge which, to her horror, her sister's actions confirmed. Ethel was holding her face up towards the man. He kissed her on the mouth, taking so long that Eileen wondered how they could breathe. When their lips finally came unstuck, they smiled at each other and, holding hands, they went towards the drawing room.

After a while Eileen crept down the stairs and stood outside the heavy wooden door. From previous attempts at listening, she knew it was not possible to hear what was being said inside but she felt she had to try. With a frisson of childlike certainty, she knew that her life was about to change.

*

Finally Miss Gray answers Bruce. 'No. I didn't like Henry Tufnell. Not one bit.' Her voice is forceful. It's the first time she has ever spoken openly of her dislike of her brother-in-law.

'Why?' The question is again softly put.

'It was bad enough when my father left. Quite horrid, in fact, but we had our home. I loved Brownswood, loved the way it was always there, always the same. Then Ethel's husband changed everything.'

'How do you mean changed everything? How could he? In what way?' Bruce knows enough about established families and manor estates to realise that christenings and weddings and funerals don't change the status quo of a well-established family, which obviously the Poundens were.

No longer able to contain himself, he rises from the chair to stretch his legs and move across the room. He finds sitting still for any length of time quite excruciating but he reckons in the circumstances it is necessary to be unobtrusive. He is a man whose body is constantly in action – if not walking from one place to the next or pacing a small space, he is using his hands extravagantly.

Now he is positioned by the side of the table, which allows him to bend sympathetically towards Miss Gray. He senses her attitude to her sister's husband could be important enough to have been one of the turning points of her life.

'He was the cause of our home and our family changing.' Her words are simple, her sadness intense.

'But how?' This is not the type of information Bruce expected. Sometimes a question will trigger a separate memory and from experience he knows that is usually the best line to pursue.

'Because he destroyed Brownswood.' Disapproval of Henry's actions snips her vowels. It's what she has thought for years but never before said.

Bruce begins to make a moue of sympathy which, in case she cannot see, he changes to an understanding cluck. Destruction seems a bit drastic but, making sure his voice sounds uncritical, he comments, 'Yes, I suppose, in the circumstances that must have put a different perspective on things.'

Miss Gray sits more upright and raises her head. 'My sister's betrothal and marriage – suitable as it may have seemed to my mother and brothers at the time – caused a lot of friction.'

Her voice trails off and Bruce wonders if she has drifted to sleep, then he has the dreadful thought that she might be dead.

He touches her shoulder. 'Miss Gray, Miss Gray. Are you all right?'

She shrugs off his hand. As though she had not stopped speaking, she continues. 'She had no right to go along with his plans, even if Henry was her husband – she should have displayed family loyalty. He ruined everything.'

Bruce is lost within the threads of her logic, which is beginning to sound like a fascinating family rift. He burns to ask precisely what her brother-in-law had done but fears if he breaks into her train of thought she could dry up. Yet he wants to encourage her flow of reminiscences. He satisfies himself with, 'Family loyalty can never be underestimated.'

'Even though I was only a child, I was devastated when he started talking about renovations. In the beginning, it was only "renovation" – that was the word he kept using. I believe my mother anticipated nothing more than minor improvements. Architecturally Brownswood was perfect as it was: a five-bay, two-storey Georgian house.'

'I like the simplicity of Georgian. It fits well into both rural and urban landscapes.'

She continues as though Bruce hasn't spoken. 'His talking about "renovation" didn't last long. He knocked down Brownswood. And then he rebuilt it.'

'How could he do such a thing?' Bruce couldn't imagine something like that ever happening within his family. Despite only owning Brown's Green Farm for a few decades, the five-bedroom turn-of-the-century dower house on the outskirts of Birmingham, bought by Charles on his return from the war, was very definitely the Chatwin family home, the core of their being. Within months his father, who worked as a lawyer in Birmingham during the week, had turned his eleven-acre holding into a working farm. His mother Margharita, no longer preoccupied with fashionable clothes and visits to the cinema, tended, killed and plucked the selection of fowl they raised and in the process lost her nerviness, while Bruce and Hugh became country children, running wild and tied to the rhythm of the seasons.

Miss Gray is speaking. 'My brother-in-law knocked down Brownswood because he felt he could. And because nobody had the courage to stop him.'

'Were you still living there while this was going on?' Bruce is beginning to suspect Miss Gray's feelings for her childhood home could be central to her life.

'No. Henry suggested it might be better if my mother and I moved permanently to our London address in South Kensington.'

She pauses, pleats at the shawl, remembering how the elaborate stucco Italianate style of the Boltons was an aggravation and a reminder to her of the simplicity and Georgian purity of Brownswood which, under Henry Tufnell's architectural management, became what later she described in her diary as 'an elaborately monstrous Victorian mansion'.

Her explanation has answered many of the questions Bruce had wanted to put to her. It has paid to remain quiet.

As though being rewarded for his silence, Miss Gray says, 'It was my brother-in-law too who pushed my mother to use her title.'

In view of her dislike of reporters and obvious reluctance to answer personal questions, the longer Bruce remained in her company the surer he was that he should not refer to her family title, which he had come across during his research. Mentally he had long crossed off the word 'title' from the list of questions in his notebook which remains firmly in the pocket of his jacket.

'My mother became the 19th Lady Gray.'

The information slips out before Miss Gray realises. As it quivers on the edge of her lips she wants to draw back the words. She doesn't know why she has spoken of the family title. From the time she understood the meaning of titles and the privileges they impose, she was opposed to them, revolting against all of what, she perceived, they stood for.

Throughout her life she has declined to use her own title. She could have had her calling cards and letterheads reading The Honourable Eileen Gray, but she didn't and she wouldn't. She refused to countenance the usage of The Honourable, despite everyone who was anyone, not only in Parisian but also in international design circles, assuring her of the benefits an English title would bring to her work.

Whenever the subject came up, she would reply crisply and in a way that precluded argument, 'No, it wouldn't. I'm Irish. And anyway it's not English. The title is ancient Scottish.' No matter how hard she was pressed about the circumstances of her family acquiring the title, she had refused to comment further.

Strange the way this afternoon is turning out. Her earlier irritation with Mr Chatwin has waned. She has made it clear to him, and like a gentleman he has accepted, that there will be no interview. It is rather pleasant having the opportunity to chat with someone with whom one feels comfortable. She explains. 'My maternal grandmother was a daughter of the 10th Earl of Moray.'

'And in old English, the name Chatwin means "a spiralling ascent",' Bruce tells her.

She likes the lightness of his interest. If he was in any way overbearing, she would have asked him to leave by now.

But she has said enough. She will not be drawn further. He will be gone shortly. And without his interview.

Old woman and young man sit in the silence broken only by the gentle spluttering of coals and the occasional purr of the cat.

'What's its name?' Bruce asks, 'The cat's?'

'He's Abelard. Perhaps he's a she. I don't know. All my cats are called Abelard.'

'Have you many?' Bruce looks around anxiously. One is bad enough.

'I think not. Just this Abelard for now. I take them in off the streets. Parisians do not look after their cats. Poor things.' There is a warmth and humanity in her voice that he hasn't noticed before.

But the subject of cats is merely an interlude.

The old mind is full of knocking memories forcing re-examination.

The young mind wonders – hopes – could he in his role of listener be edging towards the role of interviewer?

Miss Gray's open, youthful side, the side she wished for fervently but never really experienced, wants to talk out her past, to make sense of not only the major happenings but also the minor ones. She has never had the opportunity to do this – rather, she realises, she has never allowed herself the freedom to do so.

Her other part – she supposes it is her discretionary side – cautions prudence. After all, this man prowling her studio, apparently at his will, is a reporter. But a reporter, she believes, of integrity, employed by one of the most reputable newspapers in the world. Anyway, she reminds herself – and she has made it quite clear to him – that this is not an interview. It is merely a conversational exchange, although she's the one doing the talking.

Discretion, prudence and caution all played important roles in her rearing, and, for most of her life, she has adhered to them. As her mother used to say, 'It is one thing having people suspect, but it is quite another having their suspicion confirmed.'

Bruce's interviewing mind is a whirl of celebration. His instincts tell him he has broken through the layers of Miss Gray's reserve. He feels he is beginning to know this woman, in the way he came to know his grandparents and elderly relations. What he thinks of as his 'ordinary', everyday side of his mind is full of compassion for this sad, talented, lonely woman, but his instincts nudge him to handle her words with care and to respond with delicacy.

Hands folded neatly on her lap, Miss Gray nods towards the tall bookcase. One must follow one's instincts, and her instincts are good about Mr Chatwin. 'Take down the *Burke's Peerage*. It will make what I'm saying clearer for you.'

Pleased at having a legitimate opportunity to move, Bruce crosses the room, unlocks the bookcase and, reaching up to the third shelf, removes the thick leather book.

'The page is marked.'

When he opens the fine leaves at the bookmarked page, immediately his eye falls on the entry.

'Read it aloud,' she orders.

' "On the death of her maternal uncle (the Earl of Moray), 16 March 1895, she succeeded to the Barony of Gray [SCT], her right thereto being declared by the Committee for Privileges 7 July 1896. By Royal License, 7 May 1897, she and her husband took the name of Smith-Gray, instead of Smith, their children taking the name of Gray only." '

When he finishes, Miss Gray takes a small breath and begins to speak, slowly, thinking through each word, enunciating carefully, telling how her mother, on the death of the last of her uncles – there were six and all unmarried – became the 19th Baroness Gray in the peerage of Scotland.

She wasn't quite eighteen at the time but the fuss with the endless fittings for new gowns was reminiscent of Ethel's wedding, 'but understandable', as, naturally, her mother wanted them to look their best.

In order to ratify the title, her mother had to conclusively prove her claim before the House of Lords. The Boltons was buzzing with nervous excitement, and it buzzed even more when Henry visited with his lists of do's and don'ts. He wanted to ensure his mother-in-law was aware of the importance of going through with the necessary legalities.

In the end it had all worked out well. On 7 July 1896, her mother's right to the Lordship of Gray was declared by the Committee for Privileges and duly acknowledged by the Earl of Moray. She and Papa took Smith-Gray in lieu of Smith by Royal Licence – although living permanently in Italy, Papa was amenable to the change of name and indeed to family matters generally; Eileen, her brothers and sister Thora took the name and arms of Gray only; and Henry and Ethel became Campbell-Gray.

As Miss Gray finishes her explanation, she is quite astonished at the way she has opened up to a stranger about the family title. What has she said? Has she been indiscreet? No, her title is well documented but how, she wonders, could she have talked so freely?

Mr Chatwin is easy company. Although being alone has always been her preference, she has experienced too many years of seclusion. What was once creative isolation had deteriorated to the ignominy of being unknown and forgotten. Now, without ever wishing to draw attention to herself, she finds she is back in the public eye. In the beginning, the excitement of acknowledgement was quite heady but not when she discovered she was quite powerless to stop the onslaught of media attention. Publicity was never her choice. Even at the height of her fame, she hadn't courted it, she was reluctant to have anything to do with all those reporters and photographers.

The indiscretions of her contemporaries as they grow older result in ridiculous confessions, imprudent gossip, black sheep talk, as they would say in Ireland. Up to this she had considered herself above such nonsense and impervious to the ordinariness of such vulnerabilities. Now she wonders.

She expects Mr Chatwin to try to question her further, to ask for personal and family details, and if he does, she will have Louise escort him to the door.

Bruce lets rest the matter of the title, instead commenting, like a concerned friend, without the slightest hint of interrogation: 'How could your brother-in-law appear to supersede your mother and brothers?' He wonders why this intriguing Eveleen Pounden, who had the courage to elope and to marry an artist and to get on with her life when he left her, would give in to her son-in-law.

Miss Gray clucks in exasperation. 'I'm not sure, but he was impressed by lineage and proud of his background. Perhaps his reasoning was that, if my mother used her title, at the least his wife would be an honourable in her own right.'

'Where titles and money and property are concerned, that's the way many people are,' Bruce assures.

He has the shape of Miss Gray's childhood, with the shadowy figures of her family sliding to the fore; again he feels her vulnerability and all-pervading sense of loss; he believes he has gained an understanding of the private woman behind the once public persona. His heart goes out to her: for self-protection she has built an impenetrable shell around her humanity.

But her life couldn't have been all awful? He'll wager she was fun and feisty. After all, she had attended the Slade School of Fine Art. That must have taken courage? And from an early age, she appears to have travelled extensively.

'I seem to remember reading somewhere that as a young woman you spent time with your father in Italy?'

'Yes,' she says, 'they were wonderful times.'

Chapter 11

*T*he sea licked at the beige-coloured sand as Eileen walked along the seashore. She had stuffed her pale grey stockings into her boots and left them standing crookedly and slightly apart from her father's painting equipment. She touched the brim of her straw hat with the pad of her index finger, caressing its curve, and splayed her toes, wriggling them into the wave-washed sand, feeling the salty coarseness of the grains which were in sharp contrast to the powdery pinkness of the sands of Courtown Strand where Papa had taught her to swim.

For the first time on this Italian beach, which she had grown to know intimately over the years since her father had left Brownswood, she was aware of the people at play. The way they provided a backdrop to the canvas of sea and sand and sky.

The men in their prim black bathing costumes, all muscular legs and sloping shoulders; the soft curves of the young matrons modestly contained within striped bathing dresses, with frilled caps covering their hair; squealing children with boots and stockings off, skirts and breeches pulled high, full of innocent confidence; and the unsmiling nannies stifled in stiffly-starched uniforms and laced-up shoes.

By swinging her arms, Eileen sought to create her own freedom, but no amount of space could cover her embarrassment and the feelings of powerlessness she was experiencing at the blatant stares of the men. It was quite horrid. She found the stares so disturbing that she focused her gaze resolutely on the progress of her naked feet through the lapping water.

Unbeknown to her she had reached that bud stage, where she was about to step from childhood into womanhood. Not that she knew anything about the progress of this natural phenomenon, or how it would affect her, but over the past weeks she had felt differently. She was more restless and found she was spending a considerable amount of time thinking – about what, she couldn't say.

She hadn't come to any conclusions other than the sad knowledge that, even here staying with her beloved father, she had a greater desire than usual to spend time on her own. Her head felt as though it was bursting with an unfamiliar sensation, a sort of exhilaration, she decided, more exciting than unpleasant, but still unsettling. She identified it as a sort of unexplored creativity that fretted and flittered within her. As yet she hadn't been able to decide precisely what it meant, how to evaluate it or, most importantly, how to release it. And the walk wasn't helping.

She wondered if her see-sawing feelings could be related to the sorrow-tinged joy of being with her father. She had never got over the sadness of his leaving her. And now Brownswood was gone too. Other than the highly protected holidays she had spent with her family in Italy, France and Egypt, as well as her term of schooling in Germany, she knew little of the wider world or its occupants. But her childhood belief that she would be happy to live out her life in her home on the banks of the River Slaney had never wavered.

In quiet frustration, and hoping to find some sort of solace during these weeks with her father, she sought closeness with nature: the spacious freedom of the beach, the star-studded night sky and purity of dawn birdsong. Her emotions and feelings had become tied into the strange yet subtle knowledge of desire. She desired, she knew not what, and in turn she felt she was somehow desired, but she had no idea of what that involved. All she could be sure about was this craving for her own space, backed by the growing need to ensure that she could exercise control over her life.

She would not be married off by her family to someone they would judge to be a suitable Henry type. Despite Mama's pleadings, she would not conform to the expected social life of a young, marriageable, honourable in London. Her stroll through the wavelets became a stride, her small, pale feet making scandalous indentations as she kicked up sturdy splashes.

She turned back; she had walked far enough. The tail of her skirt of pale grey cotton was darkened by the sea and, although the air was hot, the water on her skin was cool enough to chill. Inhaling deep breaths of ozone, she took off her hat and gave a series of hops, skips and jumps. Her hair loosened and uncoiled from its primly clipped confines. The hot, salty breeze blowing around her head lifted and swirled strands of her hair.

The matrons and nannies recognised in her a shadow of their former carefree selves. Although now burdened with holding a family together within the conventions of the time, they were quick to sniff at her lack of decorum. Their children saw the unusual spectacle of a grown-up splashing about, behaving like one of them. Their men folk were only aware of her promise: the silhouette of her body outlined against the sky – the budding breasts, slim waist and graceful passage, as well as her sensation of rippling life and the oblivious unawareness of herself which was evident to them in her every look and movement.

In a gesture that said much about her, she threw her hat high and in a fluid movement caught it with a slapping sound between her hands and jammed it back on her head.

In the space of time it had taken her to walk some five hundred yards along the beach and back again to where her father sat painting, she had passed from being a girl with a frenzied need to sweep away the cobwebs of childhood to teetering and finally tipping over the brink into womanhood.

'I've decided, Papa. I'm going to be an artist,' she announced, flinging herself down on the sand beside his case of tubes.

James Maclaren Smith-Gray – he was still getting used to the addition of Gray to his name, but he was well used to Eileen's sweeping statements which had their own air of authenticity – had learned to keep his reactions discreet.

Without comment, he nodded. Slowly he wiped his brush on the rag sticking out from the pocket of his smock. His movements deliberate, he rested the brush in the curvature at the base of his easel before sitting down on the warm sand beside Eileen, drawing his knees to his chest and wrapping his arms around them.

He loved and was equally proud of all his children and he admired the seemingly effortless way they had fulfilled and handled the expected requirements of their heritage. But his youngest daughter remained his most beloved, and the weeks they spent together each summer had become the highlight of his life.

At Eileen's unexpected announcement, one part of him rejoiced that she wanted to follow him in his career; another part was horrified at what Eveleen and her family would make of the social implications. While painting was regarded as a suitable hobby for young gentlewomen of the time, the Pounden family were strident in their dismissal of artists and their craft. Knowing Eileen and her wholehearted approach to whatever caught her fancy he suspected she would not be content to merely dabble at being an artist.

Typically, he queried rather than commented or advised. 'What does your mother say to that? And what about Henry? How will he take to having an artist for a sister-in-law?'

'Leave Mama to me, and I couldn't care less what Henry thinks.' His daughter's voice was firm and confident.

Like a skittish racehorse, she tossed her head. Her hair was streaming down her back in a way that Eveleen would never have permitted in public. James, in keeping with his general reluctance to become involved in anything that might turn to unpleasantness, had decided that when Eileen was visiting him it was best to ignore her lack of social decorum.

Why, when, how and to where had his enchanting, loving daughter of a few months ago disappeared? She had developed a mind of her own. That's what had happened. He rather admired the thought, except when it looked as though it might lead to disagreement or confrontation with him. 'Disobedient' her mother and governess were inclined to call her behaviour. When he and his daughter were separated and living in different countries, 'feisty' was the word he used admiringly to describe her. Now that he was solely responsible for her welfare, he had no trouble applying the word 'disobedient' to her attitude and behaviour. Although no matter how easily he had been able to justify leaving his wife and children, the feeling that he'd abandoned Eileen still lurked guiltily.

With bright sunlight burnishing their heads, he looked closely at the way she was sprawled on the sand beside him. For the first time he was aware of the sensuality of her rumpled appearance, parted lips and shining wide-set eyes that seemed to reflect the moody depths of the sea. In comparison to the luscious, dark-eyed Italian women with whom he was familiar, he had worried about Eileen's physical development and her apparent lack of femininity. But that seemed to have changed. Suddenly she had blossomed. He didn't know whether to be relieved or disturbed.

'Does your mother not plan to have you presented at Court?' His question sounded hesitant.

'She does, but I don't want to, and I shan't.'

This raw forthrightness was new. It was disconcerting too. He had no experience of being on the receiving end of it. Although he had heard grossly exaggerated stories, he was sure, about her attitude to Henry's rebuilding of Brownswood. Pulling his pipe and pouch of tobacco from his pocket, he began the calming ceremony of filling, tamping and lighting. The subject of Eileen's social aspirations would be best left to her mother. He tried, 'Have you been painting or drawing, working on style or anything?'

'No. Not really. But I will. I most certainly will.' The thought of being an artist was still in embryo stage. Indeed, the idea had only come to her as she'd sat down on the sand. But the more she had thought about it during the past couple of minutes, the better it seemed as a way of forging an independent life and avoiding the ultimate maternal success of being married off like a chattel.

'Would you like me to give you some lessons in either drawing or painting, or perhaps both?' It would be wonderful to keep her with him for longer, to have her work alongside him. 'I could talk to your mother?' James' tone was hesitant; he had always bowed to his wife's wishes regarding the rearing of their children.

There was much discussion in Italy that summer about the passing of Mr Gladstone's Irish Home Rule Bill, and the shadow of London's Bloody Sunday when the police had clashed with pro-Irish Independence protestors still hung pall-like over the politics of the day. He'd read the reports and seen the illustration in the *Illustrated London News*. Being a man of peace, he'd recoiled from the violence portrayed by the black and white images. He was glad Eveleen and Eileen were no longer living in Ireland, but he wondered if his daughter, with her outspoken ways and opinions, could end up being drawn into the political unpleasantness back in London.

Eileen raised her eyebrows and looked at him. She could imagine the correspondence that would pass between her parents concerning her receiving painting lessons from her father with a view to becoming an artist. She would not get caught in their 'cross fire', as Lonsdale called their parents' disagreements.

'No, thank you. I've made up my mind. I'm going to enrol in the Slade.' Having only in that instant decided, she tossed her head and laughed at the very idea. Although the school was located in Chelsea near their London home, she couldn't remember from where she had learned about its reputation for fine art. But she was pleased with herself. Such an announcement sounded mature.

'Oh, my pet, I'm not too sure about that.' James did not want his beloved Eileen exposed to the reputation of art schools – particularly the Slade, which was considered 'advanced', with its students generally cultivating flamboyant, bohemian characteristics. The school's only-recent acceptance of female students resulted in them being thought of as 'fast new women', whatever that meant. But nothing good, he'd warrant.

'Well, I've decided, that's what I'm going to do.' Eileen jumped up as jerkily as she had sat down and stood swinging her hat, looking at her father who, having remained seated, felt somewhat disadvantaged.

There was a wild, untamed look about her that had him worried. As he wondered whether, perhaps, this was an occasion when he should admonish her or, even better, suggest they have an early lunch to take her mind off the Slade, she announced she was going for a swim.

She was eel-like in the water, strong-stroked, almost masculine in the way she cleaved through the sea in her cutting crawl, and her stamina was limitless. She swam several times a day, un-chaperoned and quite fearlessly.

Chapter 12

Confident as Eileen may have been when announcing to her father that she planned to be an artist and to attend the Slade School of Fine Art, the remainder of her family, for once united in their decision, would not condone either situation. 'Situation' was her mother's word for any form of disagreement.

Despite her best efforts, Lady Gray had failed in her many attempts to integrate her youngest daughter into society. Her suggestions of suppers, balls, outings to the theatre and house-party weekends in the country fell on stubbornly deaf ears. She threw up her hands in the air and confided to sensibly married Ethel that Eileen's behaviour bordered on rudeness; she was apparently oblivious of how important it was to the family that she should make a good marriage.

Eileen had no time for what she regarded as social frivolities. She was determinedly on a mission of wearing-down tactics. Aware of her mother's predisposition for lineage and family, she discovered that one Kathleen Bruce, of impeccable pedigree, was enrolled in the Slade.

That afternoon over tea for which she was not only on time but had dressed with unusual care, including wearing the hated whalebone-corset, she pointed out to her mother that Kathleen was the daughter of Nottinghamshire's Canon Lloyd Stewart Bruce. 'Surely if the Slade is considered suitable for the daughter of a leading churchman it wouldn't harm me or my reputation to take a few lessons? Perhaps it might even have a certain social cachet?' she asked with wide-eyed innocence, omitting to mention that Kathleen's parents were dead. By the time she had poured a second cup of tea, and was sipping decorously, she had secured her mother's permission to enrol in the Slade.

Despite Eileen's punctilious application to drawing and painting, the school did not fulfil her artistic expectations. But aware of the battle she had fought to attend, and because of her natural conscientiousness, she assiduously applied herself to the courses. Learning as much from her failures as she did from the successes of others, she set about finding alternatives for her creative ambitions.

From her days of introspection in Italy she was certain that her primary purpose in her life was to express her creativity. For months she tormented herself, wondering about the form that would best serve this. With a determinedly open mind she explored different possibilities, but none of the disciplines caught her imagination or intrigued her enough to proceed further.

Then she discovered the room full of lacquer pieces at the Victoria & Albert Museum. It was the beginning of her love affair with the medium that would last for more than two decades. The work on display was exquisite, most having been donated by Queen Victoria and the Daimyo of Satsuma, as well as a selection purchased from the Japanese exhibition at the 1867 L'Exposition Universelle in Paris, which had been decreed by Emperor Napoleon III.

She had found her creative outlet. She was sure of it. But, ever diligent, she finished out her year at the Slade while trying to locate someone to give her lessons in lacquering. When she discovered that person she would then have the difficult task of persuading the family that she absolutely, most absolutely had to learn lacquering. Nobody at the museum or the Slade could help with the name of a teacher; nobody she felt she could trust knew either – she most certainly did not want rumours circulating back to Mama before she had a solution. She never once considered giving up on her quest: instead she took long rambling, thinking walks, keeping her hunt for a teacher to the forefront of her mind.

One afternoon her resolve paid off. While wandering the streets of Soho, which because the area was expressly forbidden to her was all the sweeter for exploring, she came upon a shop front in Dean Street with a notice above the window proclaiming: D. Charles, Experts in the Art of Lacquering.

Without pausing to think of the consequences if her family dis-covered she was not only unaccompanied in Soho but also entering such premises, she pushed open the door. The scene of swirling vapour that met her was a Dante's Inferno of activity. In a fog of steam, leather-aproned men and youths leaned over small panels of wood as they applied lacquer, while others squatted awkwardly in front of larger panels. The workers paused in their strokes and raised shiny, red, wet faces to look uncomprehendingly at the unexpected intrusion.

The atmosphere was a suffocating mixture of lacquer fumes and steam. Her breath caught in her throat as she croaked, 'I wish to see the owner, Mr Charles.'

'I am Mr Charles.' A small man with a bald head and a strawberry-coloured rash spreading across the backs of his hands and up his arms came forward.

'I wish to take lessons in lacquering.' She spoke firmly.

By now she had the undivided attention of the workers, whose brushstrokes had ceased. They sat back on their hunkers, staring from her to their employer – stoat assessing rabbit came to mind.

'That's not possible,' Mr Charles spoke firmly and turned away from her.

'Wait. I will pay you.' For the few minutes she'd been in the workroom and from what she'd seen, the lacquer pieces Mr Charles's apprentices were working on looked as good to her untrained eye as those she had seen on display in the Victoria & Albert.

'I said no.' He didn't even bother to look at her.

She touched the sleeve of his shirt with her gloved hand. 'Did you hear? I will pay what you ask.' He shrugged loose and, without replying, walked to the end of the long, narrow room. His apprentices returned to their work. She had no choice but to leave.

On the next day, the day after and for many more days she returned to Dean Street. Standing tall and proud, she demanded lessons. On each occasion she was informed by a too-thin youth with a suppurating boil on his neck that Mr Charles was not in for anyone. In his thick Cockney accent, he succeeded in making 'anyone' sound a most undesirable person. On the sixth, or it may have been on the occasion of her seventh visit, Mr Charles appeared from the back of the premises.

'What do you know about lacquering?' he asked, wiping his hands on his apron.

'Nothing. That's why I want to learn the traditional Asian techniques from you.'

He stared at her, eyebrows raised, mouth slightly open, with what she took to be a look of scepticism mixed with incredulity. 'Come back tomorrow. Be here at seven o'clock. In the morning.'

She preferred not to remember the battle she had finally won late that evening with her mother. She felt no guilt about the way she had worn down the distraught older woman, pointing out how she had allowed Brownswood to be ruined and that she – Eileen – would never recover from the loss of her childhood home. But, perhaps, learning to lacquer might in some small way alleviate her sadness.

Her sole concession to her mother's concerns was agreeing to be driven to Dean Street, although the following morning she had insisted on the coachman letting her out of the carriage at the edge of Soho. Mingling among the other workers, she strode purposefully through the dawn-blanched streets which already were thick with the steady clunk of boots on stone, the wordless tramp of workers – men, women and children, pale and glue-eyed with sleep, heads down, shrouded in the smoky mist, going about their work.

By six forty-five she was waiting in the darkness outside Mr Charles's door, her reticule stuffed with money. Mr Charles hadn't mentioned the price of his classes, so she had come well prepared.

Chapter 13

Eileen may have fallen in love with Paris when she and her mother visited in 1900. However, it took several years of negotiation before she secured the permission of her family to move there permanently, but typically she had spent the intervening time well – studying various art forms but primarily learning the techniques of lacquering in the sweltering confines of Dean Street.

Finally, supported by a generous allowance and accompanied by Kathleen Bruce and Jessie Galvin, who'd been with her at the Slade, and painter Gerald Kelly, the four friends took rooms in a pension in rue de Barras, the artists' quarter near Montparnasse.

They enrolled for classes in the Académie Colarossi, the art school popular with foreign students. In the morning, models posed for genre painting, while afternoons were devoted to the practice of *croquis*, the making of rapid sketches. Students had the option of attending classes in drawing, painting, watercolour and sculpture, as well as costume and the decorative arts. Eileen settled for drawing classes, supplemented by free instruction in anatomy from the École des Beaux Arts.

After a while, she transferred to the Académie Julian, private and fee-paying, where students were trained primarily for admission to the École des Beaux Arts. The Académie prided itself on having segregated studios, yet women were taught by the same professors as their male counterparts, Jean-Paul Laurens being most notable at the time

*

'Despite my earlier difficulties with the Slade, I was delighted to be acknowledged as an accomplished artist. I knew how proud my father would be. When I was at my easel painting, I frequently felt his ghost hovering. Despite missing him terribly, I felt his guidance,' Miss Gray tells Bruce, explaining that she was particularly pleased when the additional summer classes she'd attended in Caudebec-en-Caux in Normandy resulted in one of her paintings being shown at the Salon. 'That turned out to be the achievement that somewhat reduced family opposition to my staying permanently in Paris. But my first love remained lacquering.'

'It must have been wonderful being in Paris then.' Bruce sighs, imagining the parties, clubs and soirées. 'As well as the art, all that socialising?'

She grimaces. 'I wasn't ever all that sociable, but I enjoyed my small circle of friends. Our group was creative and strangely ambitious in a relaxed sort of way. It was all very different to how things are today.'

They were good times. And like much of life, she hadn't appreciated them until they had passed. Paris was far enough away from London for her to occasionally indulge in an 'unsuitable relationship', as her mother would have described it. She enjoyed an ongoing harmless flirtation with the talented Gerald. He was the darling of critics, inspiration for the author Somerset Maugham, who regularly portrayed him in his works and a favourite with the English royal family. They had lost touch during the 1920s but she believes he was knighted in later life.

Beautiful, slender-limbed Kathleen showed a remarkable talent for sculpting. She was befriended by the sculpture Rodin – well, more than befriended, Eileen and Jessie were sure, although no matter how hard they entreated, Kathleen refused to be drawn on the exact nature of their relationship. Then, in a flurry of romance, she had married Antarctic explorer Captain Robert Scott and lost him to the snowy wastes five years later.

Jessie cared little for society or what society thought of her. She was capable of more care and love than Eileen thought possible. Cheerfully she chided Eileen for her conservative views and reluctance to face up to, what she called, the reality of 'who you truly are'. She hooted with laughter, as only she could, when Eileen confided she wouldn't want news of 'inappropriate conduct', as she defined it, getting back to her mother.

"Inappropriate conduct," Jessie spluttered, her laughter catching in her throat. 'What, pray tell, is that?'

'You know ...' Eileen's eyes would widen anxiously and Jessie would hug her, but she didn't let the matter rest.

It must have been about five o'clock on an autumn evening, just as dusk was falling and the needling rain of entire day was easing into a drizzle, when the sound of the bell floated across the courtyard. Eileen was in her bedroom attending to her latest outbreak of lacquer rash. She had already put in several hours applying lacquer and she was in a strange mood: peaceful at her progress but craving some sort of activity. She wasn't expecting anyone. When she was working on a project, most of her friends knew better than to disturb her by calling unannounced.

After the usual length of time it took for someone to reach her apartment, she heard a jumble of two voices and the blur of female sounds, followed by Louise's substantial footsteps along the corridor and her knock on the door of the bedroom. Her housekeeper's voice was flat with disapproval as she announced, 'Mademoiselle Galvin is here.'

From her first day of entering service with Mademoiselle Gray, Louise had seen her role as one of protector. The raw, young country girl had devoted herself entirely to caring for what she believed to be her mistress's frail spirit, which her rural intelligence interpreted as tormented, rather like a small songbird beating about the cruel wires of a cage.

Eileen paused from dabbing at her arms with a pad of muslin soaked in calamine lotion. What a nice surprise. 'Well, bring her in.'

'I'm not sure, Mademoiselle.' Louise's face was even more expressionless than usual, but she was saved from having to explain by Jessie's head coming around the door.

'What are you doing this evening?' Jessie bounded into the room and demanded of Eileen, who was standing by the dressing table in a lace-trimmed apricot-silk camisole. Jessie halted in her stride. 'Oh, look at your poor arms. That rash has got much worse.' She drew closer and gently ran her index finger along Eileen's clavicle. 'And it's on your neck and bosom as well. When are you going to stop lacquering?' She stood back from Eileen, a small, tight figure of indignation. 'Why can't you get Sugawara to apply the lacquer? It's a monotonous job for you, and he should be immune to the rash by now.' That was Jessie, full of concern and loyalty for Eileen but unthinking about inflicting discomfort on Sugawara.

It was only then that Eileen took in her outfit. At the best of times, Jessie had eccentric tastes in clothes, but even for her this was a step too far. She wore a three-piece, check tweed suit, complete with collar and tie, and side-buttoned spats peering out from beneath her trousers. Across her plump middle was a sturdy chain and a workman-like watch peeped from a pocket of her waistcoat. Best of all was the monocle dangling from a cord around her neck.

'Jessie, what are you up to? Where are you going?' Eileen spluttered, caught between amazement and laughter. As she took her wrap from the bed and knotted its belt around her waist, momentarily the discomfort of her rash was forgotten.

'Didn't you express an interest in visiting the Café de la Regence?'

'Yes, but what's that to do with your costume?' Eileen threw herself on the bed, laughing. Jessie joined her and like children they kicked and scissored their legs backwards and forwards, the way Eileen's sisters used to when excited.

Eileen's latest stray cat jumped up on the bed and meowed, his green eyes flat and demanding, until she picked him up. She was convinced this Abelard was an animal with a personality who liked equal measures of solitude, fun and affection. Holding him close, she tucked him under her chin and his throaty purrs echoed his approval. There was a multitude of stray cats around the rue Bonaparte and, despite Louise's sniffs of disapproval, Eileen gave many of them a home; some stayed for a few days, others remained for weeks or months, although none became permanent residents.

Jessie jumped down, puffed out her chest and drew herself up to her full dignified height, which left her at barely five feet. 'Put that cat away. We've things to do. Places to go, things to see.' She executed a little dance. 'Even you must know that unescorted women aren't allowed into the Café de la Regence, much less permitted to play chess. Come on. Hurry up. Get dressed. Put on something pretty that will act as a foil to my suit. Make sure you cover up that rash. We're going to play chess with the best.'

'I'm not sure …' Eileen stood indecisively, twirling the belt of her robe.

As Jessie moved towards her with outstretched arms, Eileen jerked backwards. Lying on the bed together kicking up their legs had been a bad idea.

Jessie stopped and stood rigidly, her plump face a study of sadness and sincerity. 'Much as I love you, Eileen, I wouldn't ruin our friendship. I've never harboured those sort of expectations from you. You should know that.'

'I do know. Sorry.' Eileen wouldn't meet Jessie's eyes. She gave a small shrug, and opened her palms defensively.

'But there's no harm in hoping,' Jessie's giddy giggle was supposed to lighten the atmosphere.

If it was possible, Eileen looked even sadder as she flicked through her wardrobe, checking for an outfit that would not be too conservative. She chose an off-white silk dress with a flared skirt and a round collar. She changed behind the screen, while the irrepressible Jessie preened in front of the cheval mirror, adjusting the line of her waistcoat and raising the legs of her trousers to admire the smoothness of her spats.

Dear Jessie was one of her most loyal friends. Because she trusted her implicitly and knew she would never break a confidence, Eileen felt relatively safe in her company on occasions, to let down her guard and be 'truly herself', as Jessie would say. But she never considered being 'truly herself with Jessie. She only gave in to her sexual urges *in extremis*; frequently her choice of partner was inappropriate and after each episode she was left with a horrid sensation of guilt.

As she brushed her hair, still behind the screen, she was bitter in her recriminations. She had misjudged the situation with Jessie this evening, jumped to the wrong conclusion. Or had she?

Eileen was attractive to both men and women and she was never without a circle of admirers. As well as being unaware of her beauty, she had an air of mystery and creative intensity which people found fascinating. Kathleen said strangers were drawn to her aloof aristocratic beauty; Jessie believed they were after her inheritance and Gerald, refusing to be drawn, just smiled rather sadly.

Eileen seldom took part in such musings. She hid behind the surety and security of creativity.

*

'I worked for several hours each day on various projects,' she tells Mr Chatwin. 'Then at the start of the war I became a volunteer ambulance driver.'

Bruce looks at her in astonishment. Miss Gray an ambulance driver? It's the last thing he expected of her. 'During the First World War, they actually allowed women to drive ambulances?'

'Yes, indeed, women were allowed to drive ambulances.' She takes a mischievous delight in stressing 'allowed'. 'Although there weren't that many of us.'

She had been one of the first women in Paris to obtain a driving licence and for several years before the war she was a familiar sight behind the wheel, motoring along the boulevards.

'It must have been traumatic.'

'Not traumatic as such. Despite the horrors of the war, they were splendid days. We, all of us, revelled in the responsibility and knowledge that we were carrying out such a vital service.'

Initially, the fact that she owned her own car, together with her rumoured title and wealth, had made her an object of envy and curiosity among the other predominantly male volunteer ambulance drivers. But she had earned their reluctant respect with her knowledge of the inner workings of engines, her driving expertise and the fearless carrying out of her duties, and that respect was sealed when they learned that she had accompanied Hubert Latham on his cross-channel flight. Latham was France's first aviation hero.

'Were you not nervous?' Bruce asks, remembering his mother's anxiety during the war, which she spent seeking safety from bombings and the like.

'No. I wasn't. Strange, I suppose, but there was so much happening that one wasn't nervous. And I was sad I had to cut short my war efforts and return to London to nurse my mother through what turned out to be her final illness.'

'That must have been difficult.' Bruce can't imagine either Hugh or himself giving up their lives to nurse their parents.

'I saw it as my duty and don't regret it.'

Duty. He should have known. Duty, it appears, was alive and well and equally stultifying in those days. This interview that wasn't an interview is constantly opening into new and exciting labyrinths of memories. And yet at any minute he expects to be dismissed. And where will that leave him?

'Although I ended up physically and psychologically drained and quite creatively bereft,' Miss Gray says.

It's a strange admission to make but she has always been glad and rather proud of the fact that she gave up her life in Paris to take care of her mother in London.

'Sugawara-san came with me to London,' she tells Bruce, wanting to somewhat deflect from the intensity of her sacrifice. 'He was delighted to have the opportunity to renew his acquaintanceship with Mr Charles and I managed to take a few advanced classes in lacquering.'

Chapter 14

Eileen's interview in British *Vogue* magazine was the most important occurrence during those months spent in London.

'A magazine of the calibre of *Vogue* expressing an interest in anyone is the ultimate accolade of artistic arrival,' pronounced Jessie, while Kathleen echoed her sentiment.

They laughed at Gerald's pomposity when he pointed out, 'Even more importantly, it heralds acceptance and awareness of you and your work by a wider public than the artistic communities.'

Eileen, feeling she had been bullied into acceptance by her friends' enthusiasm, was non-committal but privately wished she'd declined to be interviewed without telling them.

The restrictions of the war were everywhere, but Lady Gray insisted on upholding her standards. Despite the formality with which The Boltons was run, when Jessie and Kathleen called to wish Eileen luck, the three friends reverted to the casual repartee and fun of their early days in Paris. Giggling and laughing, they sat sipping tea and eating hot scones, dribbling butter down their chins while exchanging outrageous titbits of scandal.

Although the pall of Lady Gray's illness hung about the house, she had short periods when she was able to enjoy company for which she emerged from her bedroom groomed to perfection and with the freshly dressed, formal hairstyle of her youth. That afternoon was one such occasion, and she joined them for tea in the drawing room. She ignored their hilarity but expressed her displeasure at the vulgarity of her daughter's associating with 'newspaper people', as she called them. Try as they might she was not interested in their explanations that *Vogue* magazine was prestigious and could not be compared to any of the newspapers of the time.

Jessie laughed and said Lady Gray would have to grow used to having a famous daughter who'd be so celebrated that reporters would cross the Atlantic to interview her. Kathleen said all newspaper people weren't bad. Hadn't she and her young son faced the brunt of reporters' questions about her sculptures, her 'scandalous affair' and her attitude to the memory of Captain Scott? 'And we've managed to emerge relatively unsullied,' she shrugged.

The horror of the first aeroplane bombing of London, killing more than a hundred and injuring four times as many, and the King calling for a national holding back on the consumption of bread was the breakfast table conversation throughout England on the morning that Miss Madge Garland, feature writer with *Vogue* magazine, called by appointment to The Boltons to interview The Honourable Miss Eileen Gray.

Despite living in Paris, the accepted hub of avant-garde creativity, Eileen wasn't used to associating with ambitious career women whose success was judged, not on family or background, but by the money they earned themselves and the lifestyle they chose. She was unnerved by Miss Garland. The self-assured young woman, long and slender with slim ankles neatly crossed, perched on the edge of the fringed brown velvet couch. She was cool and efficient in a bottle-green cloche and tailored suit – similar in style and colour to the uniform that dreadful Countess Markievicz wore and which that season was all the rage with the young fashionable women on the streets of London.

Pen poised over notebook, the reporter looked deeply into Eileen's eyes, asked questions in a breathlessly hesitant voice and smiled brightly and encouragingly while Eileen struggled to sound confident as she sought to explain from where she drew her inspiration; what she thought about as she designed; how she created; and the way she decided on colours. All she could do in the face of such verbal onslaught was to hope she was giving comprehensible answers.

When Eileen offered the information that the inspiration for the design of a particular lacquer door panel had come from the legend of the Children of Lir, Miss Garland's breath caught in her throat and her hand faltered over the smooth flow of the black hieroglyphics of Mr Pitman's shorthand on the lined white pad of her reporter's notebook.

'But isn't that Irish?' Her eyes widened.

'Yes, it is.'

'How ever did you come across the idea?'

'I'm Irish.'

'Oh, I didn't know.' Her voice grew husky.

'What did you think I was?'

'I understood English, living in Paris.' Miss Garland injected a note of crispness into her tone. She was not a woman who wasted words. 'The Children of Lir – something about swans, isn't it?'

Eileen ignored the incredulity of her tone and kept her voice neutral. 'Yes, indeed, the story is that the children of King Lir were changed into swans by their stepmother, who was jealous of their father's affection for them.

It was the year after the Easter Rising and in the circles in which Lady Gray and her family moved there was little sympathy for Ireland or anything Irish. But Eileen was proud of her heritage. She didn't care that instead of projecting the image of an independently wealthy Londoner pursuing an artistic life in Paris, Miss Garland would see her Irish side. Despite the social freedom and creative fulfilment of her life in Paris, she still ached with loneliness for her Irish home.

Throughout the hour they spent behind the closed door of the drawing room, Miss Garland's smile was bright; she sipped coffee, holding the handle of the delicate cup with a crooked little finger. The light from the street filtered in through the lace curtains, giving her an otherworldly glow. Looking deep into Eileen's eyes, she complimented her on being the perfect interview subject. Eileen drank in her muskiness. It was the first time she'd experienced such a physical awareness of another woman. The impact of Miss Garland consolidated and confirmed much of what she'd wondered about. Her growing suspicions about who she was and who Jessie insisted she was were being confirmed.

As the butler was showing out the reporter, she doubled back to where Eileen was standing by the console table, which had its

usual arrangement of fresh summer flowers: deep-blue delphini-
ums, pale-pink lupins and crimson sweet williams, the intensity of
the blooms highlighted by the mirrored background. Eileen's heart
leapt in anticipation as Miss Garland touched her arm. But all she
said was, 'People like you and I are different. But it'll be women like
us who'll change the world.'

With a shudder of certainty, Eileen knew their moment – if they had
been fated to have one – had passed, and that Miss Garland was right.

*

Miss Gray hasn't thought about Miss Garland for decades. Why now?
What has triggered these memories? She doesn't wonder for long. She
knows: quite simply something about the ambivalence of Mr Chatwin's
personality has brought her to mind.

'Are you a full-time reporter?' she asks Bruce. 'Is reporting what
you do?' She makes her question sound as though being a reporter is a
particularly nasty occupation.

He chews on his bottom lip, although she cannot make out the
gesture, before answering, 'Well. Yes. For now it is.'

Miss Gray is torn between what she would like to do and discretion. Instinct versus prudence. Being reporters, Mr Chatwin and Miss
Garland would have much in common – she is sure he would be interested in an interview that had taken place some sixty years ago. She'd
like to tell him about it, perhaps, discuss it with him. But maybe it's
better not to. As Lizzie always maintained, sleeping dogs are best left
lying undisturbed.

She could recite the few lines from the August edition of the magazine that she'd been vain enough to learn by heart. 'Miss Gray is an artist
of rather an extraordinary sort, expressing herself with a terseness which
is almost Japanese … She stirs the imagination,' wrote Miss Garland.

Again, she thinks no. She will not.

To break the silence with Mr Chatwin, which is a pleasant quietness,
she comments, 'The destruction of war and what it does to families and
countries is unimaginable. That is, until one is caught up in it.'

Having come through two world wars and being affected by the Boer War and the Irish Civil War, she considers herself somewhat a military expert. In her opinion the youth of today don't appreciate the decades of world peace they've been lucky enough to grow up in.

Bruce doesn't agree with her. He remembers his years of war as glorious times spent with his mother, but he is pleased to be moving away from questions about him and his reporting.

Chapter 15

With the Second World War's ceasing of hostilities, the declaration of peace and the return of his father, young Bruce's life should have been wonderful, but it wasn't. The captain returned a hero. Once home he determinedly reclaimed his beloved Margharita's time and affection and Bruce lost the feeling of exclusivity he had enjoyed with his mother. He took it hard – harder than he had taken the birth of his brother Hugh – but he found a strange solace with his maternal grandfather.

Sam Turnell was a thin, melancholic man whose hobby was drawing meticulous plans of houses that he and everyone knew would never be built. As a young man he had tap-danced, galloped horses across the sands and shot grouse on the Yorkshire moors. Bruce thinks fondly of old Sam and how in some indefinable way their long walks over the moors had helped prepare him for this meeting with Miss Gray. He is experiencing an affinity, fascination and comfort with her the like of which he hasn't known since he was a young boy surrounded and chastised and loved in turn by his gaggle of delightfully eccentric elderly relations.

'Social and cultural life really took off again after the First World War, didn't it?' Bruce asks, pushing to the back of his mind – yet again – the thought of facing his editor without an interview. Magnus Linklater has no compunction about stating to anyone who will listen that, in his opinion, young Chatwin does not have the necessary training or attributes to be a successful journalist. Even worse, he described as 'arty-farty' the photographs Bruce had taken during a trip to Mauritius and which Bruce proudly believed to be true art.

But he won't think of any of that now. He is in a good place with Miss Gray, with his imagination working overtime as he conjures up visions of Paris as the epicentre of artistry and refined living. He hopes by again posing his question as a statement that she will paint a word picture of life in the City of Light – he likes the name even better than he does New York's Big Apple. Miss Gray has an understated way of talking but he has no trouble visualising what she's saying: the people she talks about have become real, their actions have purpose and their conversation is relevant, providing him a whole sequence of colourful pictures.

Bruce is magpie-like in his knowledge. The history of the First World War had always interested him more than that of the Second World War. He is particularly intrigued by the drama of the armistice: how shortly before dawn a party of Germans, including a Catholic politician and two army generals, entered a guarded railway carriage in the forest of Compiegne. Six hours later, at 11 o'clock on the 11th day of the 11th month – the wonderful synchronicity of all those elevens – in 1918, after four and a quarter years of war, the guns fell silent on the battlefields of Europe. Germany had admitted defeat and signed an armistice.

The world that stopped breathing during the war years must have started living again. He would have thought it would have happened immediately, but not according to Miss Gray.

'Social and cultural life didn't take off again after that war. Absolutely not.' In those few crisp words she has burst his bubble.

The war years of 1914 to 1918 had not stood still for her. She had found the overview of their effect to be devastating: washing over her, washing her away; leaving her feeling as though she was nothing more than a child of sand, left by a careless mother too near the water.

Between the chaos of the war and nursing her mother in London, she had been absent from Paris for a long time. Now her mother was dead, as was her eldest brother, James, who had succeeded to the title of Lord Gray on the death of their mother, but he had died unmarried less than six months later. Eileen tried not to dwell on Henry Tufnell's reaction or to imagine his gloating pleasure at the title going to her sister, his wife, Ethel. Sad and grief-stricken as she was at the deaths of her parents and brothers, for the first time in her life she no longer felt weighed down by the burden of duty.

When she had returned to Paris, the city she had known was changed. That summer sweltered in a ferocious heat wave which had hot steam hissing from the wet rings left by wine glasses on the steel tables of the outdoor cafés, and sometimes their interiors could resemble a battleship stripped for action.

It wasn't called the Great War without reason. More countries were involved and more people perished – over ten million – than in any previous single conflict. Three-quarters of a million men from Britain died. The price of victory for France was even greater; despite its smaller population, its death toll was almost twice as high.

Initially the concept of war had been lauded by members of the artistic community as 'the great remedy' and the 'cleansing', with the Futurists glorifying it as 'the world's only hygiene'. The question that hovered sometimes unasked, more times unanswered, was how to rebuild society after the devastation of war. The creative people and literary tourists of the time believed the arts could be the foundation for restructure. Full of the extravagant patriotism of cultural immigration, they gathered in cafés to gossip and slander and savour the old tales of lost generations while bemoaning the state of the country and, even worse, the state of the city. But, strangely, despite the devastating après war economics, this restructuring took place with a lavishness not seen for generations. Paris of the 1920s became a hedonist's delight.

But one would have had to have lived through the experience to appreciate it …

'Surely you were able to take up with your friends and work where you'd left off before the war?' Bruce probes. He is trying to find a tactful way to ask her about her personal life. She must have had relationships. With her talent and looks, she had to have been the toast of Paris. Well … one of them, anyway.

He has seen photographs of her and is particularly intrigued by the hauntingly mysterious study by New York-based photographer Berenice Abbott.

Since Miss Gray's rediscovery, this particular photograph may have become over-used, but Bruce believes it captures her spirit – the haughtiness, creativity and mysteriousness. She would have had that quality to 'knock one for six', as he had described his first meeting with the gorgeous Ivry Guild, sister of his best friend Raulin at Marlborough College. Bruce believes people never forget their first taste of lurking sexuality, particularly when it is masked with glamour and sophistication. He certainly hasn't.

As though it is only yesterday, he can remember the sunny summer Sunday afternoon when Ivry motored down to the college from London, accompanied by the film producer who had written *The Red Shoes*. Dressed like a 1920s flapper, she slid out of a two-tone Bentley and from the boot she unpacked chocolate cake, smoked sturgeon and fresh horseradish cream.

In advance of her visit, Raulin told Bruce that he had sung his praises to his sister, assuring her he was 'a most fascinating man'. Afterwards she told her brother that she'd found Bruce 'vital and intensely bright'. She was Bruce's first taste of glamour and sophistication, his first love and one of the few people he knew in London during his early days with Sotheby's. He kept a photograph of her in his jacket pocket, and it was no secret to his friends that he planned to ask her to marry him, although he fretted about being four years her junior. Like many of the girls he took a fancy to, he never put his feelings into words, and so she never knew of his plans for her.

'What do you mean – friends and work?' Eileen Gray's voice sounds irritable. Quite suddenly she finds she is tetchy at the relentlessness of her memories. It is the fault of this young Mr Chatwin. That's the problem with people like him who are reporters. Nice and pleasant as they may be, after a while of listening they have to blunder in, asking these ridiculous questions. She should insist he leaves. She will. But first she'll have to correct his misconceptions. One can't have a reporter running around with mistaken beliefs.

'After that war and the damages it wrought, nothing could ever be the same again. Everything was changed.'

Post war, there was that awful sensation of controlled hysteria throughout Paris. Eileen tried to fit in, to enter into the spirit of change. To lighten up, she supposes would be the phrase used today. She attributed her artistic streak to her father and credited her mother with her aristocratic sense of self and awareness of proper behaviour. Her attributing and crediting was done gaily and in a contrived lighthearted manner. With the breaking down of the social barriers of the masses, she could be embarrassed by her impeccable pedigree.

But then everything in her life changed. She met Damia, nightclub singer and club owner.

Chapter 16

*N*ever will Eileen forget her first sight of the dazzling, scarlet-lipped woman. With her elbows propped on the small round table and her voice confident, she was holding forth on the importance of the 'choreography of staging' to the rapt audience of aristocratic-looking men and their glamorous women.

Eileen wasn't sure what 'choreography of staging' meant, but she was sure about the shivers running up and down her back, the familiar way her belly tightened, as it did on momentous occasions, and the ridiculous certainty that her life was changed, that it would never be the same again.

'Who is she, who is that?' Eileen had whispered to Jessie, who had dragged her reluctantly to Montmartre. She disliked clubs but Jessie said the ambiance of Concert Damia and its singer, who was known throughout Paris as *La Tragedienne de la Chanson* because of the despair and misery at the core of her repertoire, would perfectly suit her mood. Eileen, aware of the air of melancholy that was folded around her like an envelope, had given into Jessie rather than argue.

'That's Damia, that's her.' Jessie was well enough known in the club to have secured a prime table near the stage.

The woman known as Damia stood up, pushing back her chair with practised insouciance, stretching to her full magnificent height while alternatively sipping from a glass of champagne and using a cigarette holder to gesticulate, as she pontificated, laughed and flirted. She was a handsome figure in a black sleeveless V-neck dress. When it was patently apparent that every eye was upon her, that she dominated the club, she moved slowly across the floor, weaving in and out through the tables, pausing here to touch a shoulder, stopping there to shake a hand, everywhere to give and to receive social kisses.

The jut of her breasts, tightening of her buttocks and throw of her head ensured she remained the focus of attention as she climbed the three steps to the small stage with the sweep of black velvet curtains.

As the milky spotlight carried out its trial run, she carried out a last-minute check with her accompanist, the silhouette of her body leaning towards the shadowy figure seated at the piano heightening tension, anticipation and mystique. From its opening night, during the early months of the war, Concert Damia was the place to be seen.

As she came forward, slinking slowly across the stage, she made every hip movement count. With her head thrown back and her hands relaxed by her side, Damia paused, waiting for the spotlight. Before singing a single note, she had her audience mesmerised, and none more than Eileen. Finding Damia, the spotlight caressed the sharp bob of her dark hair, white column of her neck, bare arms and hands, lingering down the perfection of her simply clad figure.

Eyes half closed and hips swaying gently, she started with 'C'est mon Gigolo' and moved onto 'Johnny Palmer'. Eileen sat motionless, her chin cupped in her palm, watching hungrily, wondering who she knew who she could ask to introduce her to Damia.

As the singer finished with 'Les Goélands', Jessie leaned across the table. 'Shall we invite her to join us for a drink?'

*

She will not revisit her Damia days with Mr Chatwin. Their relationship was not for sharing. Those times were sacrosanct.

And it is not only her relationship with Damia that she has chosen to keep private. Some years ago, determined not to leave behind any personal records, she had enrolled Louise's help and between them they had destroyed her personal papers, letters, billets and photographs.

The fire splutters and spits on a slatey knob of coal.

She may have fought long and hard to excise and relegate such memories to the past, but she hasn't succeeded. No matter how hard one tries, one can't burn reminiscences. They have a habit of intruding, and this afternoon there appears to be no way of getting away from them.

*

Shy at the best of times, Eileen was utterly tongue-tied when Damia joined them after her performance, laughingly and delightedly accepting the applause and shouts of 'bravo' as her due. Luckily Jessie carried the conversation, her bright eyes lively as she chattered gaily about Eileen and her success – that was Jessie: big and generous hearted.

Eileen, feeling the draw of Damia's attention, gradually thawed as they discussed the properties of absinthe, while Jessie, quiet now, watched and listened: Damia's interest in Eileen was evident in the way she leaned in towards her, caressed her hand as Eileen lit her cigarette, and her silent toasting, with coquettish eyebrows rising above the rim of her champagne glass.

As she stood up from their table in preparation for her second show of the evening, again she had the undivided attention of her patrons and her dark eyes were wide and fixed in anticipation of her performance. Already tuned in to her audience, she was losing awareness of anyone or anything that wasn't pertinent to her act, although she turned slightly and paused long enough to say, 'I will see you afterwards.' Her glance encompassed Eileen more than Jessie.

'No,' said Jessie. 'By the time you're finished, we'll be gone.'

Eileen was too stunned to say anything as Jessie bundled her from the club and into a waiting cab.

'Why did you do that?' Eileen demanded.

'To save you from yourself and Damia, although I suspect I may be too late.'

Jessie was right. Eileen's obsession with Damia had been instant and all-consuming and it was already ground into her bones.

From the beginning, she was aware that her intensity of feeling wasn't reciprocated. But she didn't care. She suspected if she revealed the extent of her emotional involvement it could over-whelm the precarious balance of their connection – and throughout their relationship it remained precarious. But the stirrings she felt for the singer were stronger than she'd experienced with any of the men she'd allowed into her life – or, indeed, the women. Her acceptance of her bisexuality brought awareness that knowledge is not always a conscious thing – it can reside for a long time in the secrecy of the human heart.

In those early days, being near Damia was enough for her, and as a token of her love and commitment she gifted her six lac-quer chairs – the *sirène* chairs as they became known, depicting a mermaid embracing a seahorse. By then, throughout Europe and beyond, Eileen Gray was regarded as one of the most visible pro-ponents of art deco. However, her style, as illustrated by *Le Destin* and other pieces commissioned by Jacques Doucet, was not the usual geometric cubist, but rather a human, exotic organic style. The humanity shown in her work was different to the cool detach-ment of the prevailing trend towards functionalism and, indeed, to her public persona.

The gift of the chairs was Eileen's quiet, understated way of acknowledging and endorsing their love affair. But it hadn't been enough to make Damia exclusively hers. She wasn't monogamous and she refused to be monogamous, something Eileen had great difficulty accepting. Equally, she knew Damia was more commercial than cre-ative and, unless money was involved, she had little appreciation for the finer points of art or culture. Eileen grew to know her as a collec-tor knows his butterflies: beautiful samples pinned in glass cases, wings outstretched so that every marking is clear. By checking the nuances of Damia's light and shade, each laugh and sigh, the gentle susurration of her successes, she came as close as she dared.

Eileen's tight, protective circle of friends regarded her relationship with Damia as 'inappropriate' or 'disastrous', depending on who was commenting. But they all presumed and hoped it was just another of Eileen's quickly passing fancies. Where her sexual relationships were concerned she was more comfortable shying away from the upper classes of her birthright: choosing the daughter of a gendarme as her lover was in character, although her openness and her obvious delight in their relationship was not, and it was generally felt that Damia's blatant ambition could only be detrimental to Eileen's happiness.

From an early age Damia was determined to be a singer. Her first mentor was Robert Holland, a leading singer/songwriter who provided her with voice training and lessons in staging and who became so besotted with her that he left his wife. Damia wasn't interested in his prowess as a lover, and he was generous enough with his money, but despite it being known that she was his mistress and spoken of in cabaret and nightclub circles as having talent, she rose no further than second billing on any of his programmes.

That changed when she met Loie Fuller. The ageing American pioneer of modern dance and revolutionary theatrical lighting techniques was regarded as the embodiment of the Art Nouveau movement, and respected by the likes of Rodin and Toulouse-Lautrec. She promised to make Damia a star. It was an offer Damia could not and would not refuse, and she would do anything – well, almost anything – to achieve it. Her interest in Robert waned as Loie inducted her into stage presentation and performance art. The use of a spotlight and the sleeveless black sheath V-neck dress became her signatures. She learned fast – networking, Miss Gray believes, would be the modern word. She had no compunction about using everyone and every ploy to further her career. Her voice was strong and powerful and seductive, and she mastered the art of diction in a way that captivated her audience. Being graceful and big-boned, she had an indefinable presence, never more so than in her club.

The sensory memories of Damia are as strong now as they were all those decades ago. In those days Eileen could sense her presence; know her by the scent of sex that hung in abundance about her; the way her body tingled at her proximity; she knew the taste of her better than she wishes to recall; and the delight at seeing her – those sinuous, strong-shouldered movements, dark hair and broad capable hands chopping at the air in description.

Each night and with each performance, Damia gilded her reputation further as the most important exponent of the *chanson realist*. From her vantage point in the grey darkness, Eileen watched Damia perform, knowing she existed only for herself and the throbbing, swaying power that her voice and words held over her audience, wondering would they be together that night. Her happiness was the anticipation of happiness, and her happiness overflowed on the occasions when Damia spent the night at rue Bonaparte. She ignored Louise's stony disapproval.

The following morning they'd rise as late as Eileen could bear, but not before loving and laughing in the rumple of sheets and tangle of pillows, Damia wrestling Eileen until she had her enveloped in her strong white arms, refusing to allow her to go to her workroom. Damia hated mornings and by keeping her eyes shut and the shutters closed over she would pretend it was still night. She only came alive after noon and did not function until she had drunk several extra-strong bowls of coffee. Eileen on the other hand was a dawn riser, and she did her best work either in the early hours of the morning or late at night. As a couple their circadian rhythms couldn't be more incompatible. They were mismatched in other ways too – more incompatible than compatible – although Eileen determinedly centred on their harmony.

With Damia's pet cheetah on a leash, they'd wander along the rue de Faubourg Saint Honoré, stopping off at some fashionable café for coffee. Initially Eileen was embarrassed by the attention they received, and, with bent head, she would retreat into the background. As she was invariably holding the cheetah, she had little chance of remaining anonymous or of distancing herself from Damia's celebrity status. Damia was so animated and extroverted that it was difficult not to be caught up in her enthusiasm as she dispensed joyous smiles and warm handshakes, assuring everyone within earshot how happy she was to have the opportunity of meeting her public during daylight hours.

Sometimes of an afternoon – when it seemed the sun always shone from a blameless blue sky – they'd drive up and down the Avenue Champs-Élysées with the cheetah stretched across the back seat of the motor and Damia sitting in front with Eileen. With the fringed tail of her scarf flying in the soft breeze and her hand resting on Eileen's knee, she would sing loudly and teasingly and over-dramatically 'Tu ne Sais pas Aimer', and Eileen would smile her secret smile and pretend not to notice.

The avenue was Eileen's favourite street. She loved its exclusive shops, polite bustle and the lines of clipped horse-chestnut trees along its pavements, and she was intrigued by the source of its name: Elysian Fields, the place of the blessed, according to Greek mythology – '*La plus belle avenue du monde*' – for her it truly was the most beautiful avenue in the world.

Melting with desire, Eileen tried valiantly to meet her lover's needs by turning away from her drawing board and sitting for endless hours in endless nightclubs. Commissioning the delightful Paul Poiret, who was the toast of stylish Parisian women, to create brocade outfits suitable for nightlife gaiety, she entered as fully as she could into the spontaneous, crazy escapades that invigorated Damia and drove her act to new heights of passion. Such behaviour was anathema to Eileen. Despite the impulsiveness of her creativity, she was happiest with an orderly life – with punctuality, regular meals and appointments carefully entered in her diary.

She came to realise that Damia was and always would be only truly at home in Concert Damia. Night after night between performances, she held forth in her deliciously ridiculous way, expounding on a diversity of subjects such as Freud's talking cure, Coco Chanel's latest lover, the price of melons – whatever subject took her fancy or was the topic of the masses about which invariably she knew little. And Eileen watched the swirl of smoke from Damia's cigarette looping outwards and upwards as she entertained the revellers, tipsy and sober, who were drawn to her company like moths to the light.

Plump little Loie Fuller became a constant presence. Brash and over-confident, she styled herself as Damia's manager and made no secret of her attraction to the singer, announcing in her grating voice how they had an instant connection. She let everyone within earshot – and probably beyond – know she was nurturing Damia's talent and taking care of her health.

Eileen didn't trust Loie but she had to admit that she was full of innovative ideas about 'branding' and creating 'added value' before the words, much less the concepts, had become part of anyone's lexicon. Eileen listened while Loie outlined plans and strategies. Occasionally Damia turned to her and, widening her eyes, a habit she had when looking for confirmation of one of her statements, she asked, 'Do you agree, *ma chérie?*' When Eileen believed Damia's need for agreement was directed solely towards her, she was flattered. However, as she discovered, frequently it was no more than an endearing ploy, Damia's way of drawing people in to her circle – she had a great need to be the centre of attention.

Eileen was jealous of the closeness between Damia and Loie, although she was comforted by the knowledge that Loie was in a long-term relationship. Her live-in companion was Gabrielle Bloch, daughter of the wealthy banking family who headed up an international consortium. She dressed in a series of men's sombrely styled suits and was the recipient of a substantial allowance from her father with the proviso that she lived her life discreetly.

*

Eileen shakes her head at the poignancy and strength of love. All those years ago and the memories of Damia remain as potent as though it had all happened yesterday. Their liaison was short and intense. She could trace the beginning of its decline to when Gabrielle began coming to Concert Damia. She was unpleasantly caustic in manner, doughy-faced and silent with black button eyes, ever watchful. Eileen had a bad feeling about her, and she wasn't the only one: nobody in their group warmed to her. After their first meeting Damia had announced gaily, 'Gabrielle Bloch's only recommendation is her family's wealth.'

Some months later, Eileen was more saddened than angry, although not too surprised, when, after Loie's sudden death from pneumonia, Damia and Gabrielle became lovers. Despite knowing and slowly accepting that the passion of unrequited love was unsustainable, she was upset by the indecent haste with which they set up as a couple.

What a waste of love. Damia went from success to success, making films, starting with the silent *Napoléon*, followed by her best known *Sola* and *Notre Dame de Paris*, where she played alongside a Hollywood actor called Anthony Quinn. Eileen's sigh is as much for herself as for Damia: despite living a short distance from rue Bonparte they didn't speak for decades, and for the past twenty years she has been interred in the Cimetière de Pantin.

Around the time of the breakdown of her relationship with Damia, she had more worries. She touches her eyeglasses, adjusting them on the prow of her nose.

'You have a problem with your sight?' Bruce asks in a kindly way. He has watched her wrapped in quietness and sensed sadness. His question is not only out of context: it is the first truly personal question he has asked. Her hand touching the frames of her glasses had triggered it, spontaneously. He wishes he had remained quiet, but when she begins speaking he is glad he didn't.

'Yes. My eyesight has been a problem for a long time,' she says. 'It has been deteriorating since the1920s. I had bouts of blurring and reduced vision. I travelled for consultation all over Europe to the top opticians and ophthalmologists. No one was able to make a firm diagnosis or offer a solution but they all projected eventual blindness.'

She has his undivided attention now. He is no longer thinking of anything but her; no longer worrying about Mr Linklater's reaction to the lack of an interview. What they have in common is quite extraordinary: they are loners with eye problems, have needy relationships with their fathers and have lived in similarly named houses – Brownswood and Brown's Green Farm. He senses there is more.

She continues explaining how the deterioration of her sight was gradual but relentless, while the lenses of her spectacles grew thicker and thicker – although she points out she was grateful for the mercy of being able to continue with her work. Then when least expected her vision appeared to level out. A year later she became blind in one eye.

'Since then, I've been lucky. There has been little further decline in the sight of my good eye.'

Lucky, she says. Blind in one eye wouldn't be his idea of luck. He doesn't comment because he is not sure what to say.

Before dismissing Mr Chatwin, she decides, she'll tell him about the rue Lota apartment. It was one of her first design successes. And he is such an appreciative listener.

Chapter 17

When Eileen had returned to Paris after the war, Jacques Doucet had recognised the bleakness within her and sensed she was a lost child to creativity. After buying *Le Destin*, he had appointed himself as her unofficial mentor: publicly praising her and her work, organising showings, interviews and photographic sessions, as well as ensuring her name appeared on the right guest lists. In the beginning she had found his interest somewhat irritating and condescending, but she had come to recognise the integrity and value of his mentorship. He was a prime example of the good and honourable winning out and they became firm friends.

He ignored her brave assurances about the time she had spent in London and set about rekindling her enthusiasm, reminding her of her talent and appealing to her ambition. When his words seemed to be falling on barren ground, over a glass of wine in Les Deux Magots, conjuror-like he produced his trump card: to make a presentation to Madame Levy for the refurbishment of her rue de Lota apartment.

Eileen wrinkled her nose and shrugged. She found it difficult to enthuse about anything to do with Madame Levy. She was a social-ite and wife of Eugène Levy – a wealthy banker more than double her age who, rumour had it, she knotted round her little finger – as well as the owner of the celebrated *salon de modiste*, which she had acquired from a friend of Jacques Doucet. She was better known as Suzanne Talbot and it was through his auspices that Eileen had been admitted to this discerning, rather tight-knit circle – not that she was interested in acceptance in any social circle, tight-knit or not.

Eileen hadn't told Jacques that her interest in lacquering was beginning to wane: quite simply, she had achieved what she'd wanted and it no longer challenged her creativity. As yet, she hadn't replaced lacquering with anything else.

Jacques ignored Eileen's lack of enthusiasm as he pressed home his point: she would be able to work on her own and have complete control of the project. 'Creative freedom,' he dangled the words temptingly – as well as the refurbishment and décor throughout, this would include her design of furniture and lighting. He knew better than to mention the word 'fee'.

For the first time in months, she could feel her creative juices begin to flow. 'The whole apartment, not just lacquer work?'

'Yes,' he answered simply.

She raised her glass and smiled. This could be the project she was waiting for, the one that would allow her to spread her creative wings.

As she set out for her first meeting with Madame Levy, she was as excited as she would allow herself to be. The thought of redecorating a complete apartment was heady. But her cautious nature ensured that she reserved judgement until she had seen the apartment before allowing her hopes to be raised.

Wearing a slender calf-length skirted suit in charcoal grey with a long lean jacket and elegant court shoes, she moved briskly through the district of her beloved Saint-Germain des Prés. It was a long walk to rue de Lota but she had allowed plenty of time. She enjoyed walking and it was while walking that she came up with some of her best and most creative ideas.

That morning a sky the colour of school ink hung over the city. The air smelled sharp, slicing low around the angles of buildings. Occasional slanting shafts of sunlight dragged shadows out onto the pavements where café society thrived and intellectual aspiration simmered. A selection of preliminary sketches, notes of various ideas and samples of materials for Madame Levy's apartment project were neatly clipped together in a smart satchel with big buckles and a long strap which she had slung over her left shoulder.

Despite her proposed client being one of Paris's most successful milliners, Eileen was hatless. She had spent at least ten minutes locked in deep debate regarding the diplomacy of wearing her newest cloche. 'Will I?' 'Won't I?' She ruminated backwards and forwards, putting on and taking off the hat and looking in and out of the mirror before deciding no. She liked the comfort of her shingled hair, and privately she was pleased at the flattering way the cut defined her features, although what appealed most was the freedom from the weight and complicated dressing that her long, thick hair had necessitated.

Now that she was back in Paris, Eileen had grown to love the architectural grandeur of her adopted city with renewed passion. She never ceased to be enchanted at the way the misty street lamps marked the Pont Neuf; the power of the imposing Gothic bulk of the Préfecture; the wonderful, unique wedge of the Place Dauphine; and across the river, perched on the Île de la Cité, lay the enormous flaming jewellery of Notre Dame's stained-glass windows.

She was nervous about this meeting, clutching and un-clutching her hands, aware of what felt like a swarm of fluttering butterflies at the base of her belly. Pausing on the pavement, she straightened and softened her shoulders and neck; with chin pointing downwards and feet hip width apart she began the calming technique she had learned from Sugawara: breathing in slowly through her nose, she pushed out her belly, held her breath then breathed out through her nostrils while snapping back her belly. Having established the rhythm of her breath, she began walking again.

After all, she hadn't got the commission yet, and she couldn't be sure it would be for her.

Following the most cursory viewing of the perfectly proportioned rooms, Eileen knew this apartment was the ideal site on which to realise her designs. Without comment to Madame Levy, a soignée brunette whom she found overly forceful and synthetically poseur-ish, she envisaged a total strip out, with walls pared back to bare plaster and floors sanded to their original boards before implementing the rich frugality of her plans.

As well as being commercially astute, Madame Levy was a design visionary with a keen understanding of the power of publicity. From her first cursory but all-embracing look at Mademoiselle Gray's drawings and samples, she had recognised the potential of the innovative design which was being presented to her. Not that she would ever be lavish in praise.

'These are interesting,' she announced, straightening up from a brass-inlaid table after spending several minutes re-thumbing through the sketches.

Eileen remained standing, unnervingly statuesque. She did not comment.

'I am impressed by the rigour of your preliminary drawings.'

The slight incline of Mademoiselle Gray's head reassured Madame Levy that she had heard, but when she didn't say anything she busied herself further studying the samples of colour and material, testing the quality by running her fingers across surfaces and holding up the swatches of material to catch the light. 'I like the way you've masked luxurious style behind simplicity.'

Still Eileen did not comment nor did she make any attempt to converse. As a cover for her shyness, which was still in evidence when she was among strangers, she feigned a blasé, laconic approach. Her public persona was one of wealthy, pampered confidence which, with the exception of 'wealthy', couldn't be further from the truth.

From various entertainments and social gatherings they had both attended before the war, Madame Levy had decided that Mademoiselle Gray's personality was more introvert than extrovert and that she was quite lacking in social graces. With the amount of money at stake and the honour of being considered for the refurbishment of her apartment, Madame Levy felt she could at least make an attempt at polite conversation.

Well, if Mademoiselle Gray wouldn't converse, she would certainly ask the questions for which she wanted answers. She knew better than to query any aspects of the design, and dear Jacques had suggested at this stage, and in the circumstances, as he had delicately put it, the subject of money or fees should not be mentioned.

'How long do you envisage the job will take?' While Madame Levy craved the most fabulous and talked-about apartment in Paris, she wished to be as little discommoded as possible.

'As long as is necessary.'

The reply was delivered crisply enough to stir Madame Levy to ignore Jacques's advice and ask, 'And what about the overall price of the completed job? Do you have the figures on that yet?' While her stocks of stylish hats were in the latest designs and colours, the success of her business was primarily due to the tight rein she kept on expenditure.

Eileen thought in terms of design and colour and texture. She never budgeted or took into account the amount of money involved in a project. She felt if someone had to ask the price of something, they most likely couldn't afford that something.

'Not at all,' Mademoiselle Gray replied.

'When will you have the financial breakdown?'

'I won't.'

A quick look at her autocratic demeanour changed Madame Levy's mind about pursuing the cost of the refurbishment. From her dealings with titled society, she knew there was something powerfully impenetrable about the veneer of protectiveness bestowed by a title, particularly a British title dating back hundreds of years. No wonder Mademoiselle Gray was the talk of the city. Thankfully, money for the refurbishment of the apartment was not a problem and she would not allow dearest Eugène to make it one.

Madame Levy didn't let the negatives of life intrude. 'Do sit down,' she urged Eileen, gesturing towards a buttoned chair upholstered in dull brocade, 'and I'll ring for tea.' Being English, she knew that Mademoiselle Gray would be a tea rather than a coffee-drinker.

She pulled on a bell rope and, determined to play hirer with hired she draped herself across a chaise-longue and crossed her ankles before inserting a cigarette into a long ebony holder. Her small white hands with their bitten nails made a production of lighting the cigarette. She smoked in silence for what seemed an age, as the bell wasn't answered, and Mademoiselle Gray remained standing.

With a flounce of her skirt, Madame Levy stood up, crossed the room back to the table holding the sketches and began thumbing through them again. She would deal with the maid later.

Gleefully she anticipated the international newspaper and magazine coverage her completed apartment would generate. It would be a work of art, a showpiece, the like of which up to now, even in Paris, was unprecedented. But she knew the designer could, and did, pick and choose what appealed to her, and from her attitude she feared Mademoiselle Gray might only be making her presentation as a favour to Jacques. Close as she and he were, she had heard that he and Mademoiselle Gray were even closer.

In that she was partly right, but Eileen and Jacques's closeness was only of the creative variety and once Eileen had seen the possibilities and potential of the Levy apartment, Monsieur Doucet's work was done. She wanted the assignment as much as Madame Levy wanted her – she could feel the watering of creativity at the back of her mouth. Not that any of this was obvious from her courteous poise. Despite unfounded rumours of her design ability, she was not experienced in making presentations, but her skill at handling herself, the job and her client was instinctive.

The two women remained at silent impasse. When Madame Levy stood back from the sketches, Eileen gathered them up and tidily piled the samples on top. Madame Levy took a few puffs of her cigarette and said, 'My husband and I would want you to start as soon as possible and finish as quickly as possible. We dislike being inconvenienced.'

As there was no sign of a servant or tea, Eileen began packing the sketches and samples into her satchel.

'You may leave them. I wish to show them to Monsieur Levy this evening.'

'Everything remains with me until the contract is signed.' Eileen thought of how proud Jacques Doucet would be as she parroted the words he had insisted she learn.

Chapter 18

*N*ext morning, with her head full of plans for the rue Lota apartment and an enthusiasm and determination dating back to her *Le Destin* period, Eileen made a list of priorities. With coffee at her elbow and cigarette between her fingers, she assessed the time required and the amount of work involved for completion of the final drawings. That done, she trawled through her contact book sourcing the materials and craftsmen she planned to employ to make up her designs; after that she contacted various tradesmen, but only those with proven experience in the skills required for the job. From start to finish she would oversee personally every aspect of the work.

*

'The rue Lota project was the start of my preoccupation with block screens. I saw them as both a decorative and functional medium. I loved their striking inventiveness and the versatility of their free-standing designs, which bridged the gap between furniture, architecture and sculpture,' Miss Gray tells Bruce. 'I used them to create an intimate and exotic setting for the mix of lacquer furniture and tribal and ancient art which the Levys collected and which would form part of the refurbishment.'

'Were you nervous starting such a big project?'

She thinks for a moment and her smile is startling. 'Yes, I was. Terrified, I suppose, that it wouldn't come up to my expectations.'

From what he has learned of her, Bruce is not surprised that her priority was fulfilling her criteria rather than those of the clients and that her attitude was one of perfectionism.

*

The key to Eileen Gray's scheme for the apartment was to cover the walls with lacquered panels decorated with linear sweeps similar to those she had used on the reverse side of *Le Destin*. In the long hallway she used four hundred and fifty small, rectangular, veined panels, lacquered in black and textured with eggshell, giving the appearance of a latticed screen set like bricks against the walls; halfway along the hallway the panels opened out perpendicular to the wall into screens which broke up the over-long space.

She covered the floors with large, thick black carpets punctuated with abstract motifs borrowed from Cubism and its rhythms. The carpets were designed by her and made up in her rug-making workshop in rue de Visconti, overseen by her American friend Evelyn Wyld, who was an expert in weaving and knotting, thanks to the time she and Eileen had spent in Morocco learning the techniques and the use of natural wool dyes from Arab women.

The lighting throughout the apartment was muted, with the majority of the fittings in glass and chrome.

Her furniture included a black lacquer desk raised on arched legs with carved ivory drawer handles; a sleek low bookcase in dark-brown lacquer; a tub armchair in red and yellow lacquer, with armrests modelled as the sweeping lines of two serpents; and a dressing-table of sycamore and ivory.

Her supreme invention and essence of extravagant elegance was the *Pirogue* sofa, shaped like a dug-out canoe in silver leaf and contrasting textured, brown lacquer which resembled the pelt of an otter; it was raised on twelve arches and stuffed with matt-gold cushions. This sofa was a form without precedent in the history of furniture design, and some two years later it was where Baron de Meyer, the photographer of the day, chose to photograph Madame Levy.

Even before the apartment was finished, as Madame Levy had anticipated, it attracted considerable attention in international newspapers and magazines. In September 1920, *Harper's Bazaar* published a feature titled 'Lacquer Walls and Furniture Displace Old Gods in Paris and London'; two years on in *Les Feuillets d'Art*, the Duchess of Clermont wrote an article called 'The Lacquer Work of Miss Gray'. Although she did not specifically identify the Levy apartment, she discussed the precise achievements of its interior. Further press attention came from *The Times* and the *Daily Mail* in England and the *New York Herald* and *Chicago Tribune* in the States. Eileen Gray was providing finishing touches up to 1924, and the continuing publicity was beyond Madame Levy's wildest dreams.

*

'What a wonderful achievement – I wish I could have seen the apartment in all its glory. And the media attention – although I suppose that didn't interest you.' Bruce gives a little laugh. 'I hope Madame Levy was suitably impressed and grateful.'

Miss Gray doesn't comment.

*

As Eileen had set out to make her presentation to Madame Levy, never for one moment did she consider the impact that one project would have on her career. Even before completion it had caused as much, indeed more stir, than *Le Destin*. She could not have foreseen, either, the number of titled Europeans, American millionaires, Argentinean beef barons and Indian princes who would clamour for her designs.

Nor when the apartment was finally finished could she ever have conceived that a decade later the spaces she had so lovingly created would be redesigned by architect Paul Ruaud, who would re-orchestrate the rooms as a symphony in white with a floor of frosted glass. He used her screens – now painted white – her Pirogue sofa and Serpent and Bibendum chairs as props in what turned out to be a theatrical style setting, which was the opposite of her approach to creating living spaces. When pictures of the rooms were published in 1933 in *L'Illustration*, her part in the refurbishment was not even acknowledged.

The story of the rue Lota apartment is one of the examples of joy converting to sorrow that she prefers not to dwell on.

*

1922 was a year of firsts. The treasures of Pharoah Tutankhamun, dating back 3,000 years, were unearthed in Egypt's Valley of the Kings by archaeologist Howard Carter, who described them as 'Many wonderful things'. Spice was added to the Parisian air with the publication of a limited edition novel titled *Ulysses* by Dubliner James Joyce. And Mademoiselle Eileen Gray opened Galerie Jean Désert, sited at 217 rue du Faubourg Saint Honoré.

Bruce has seen pictures of the striking but simple façade of the gallery, and he is particularly impressed with the sculptured baroque stonework exterior and the first floor's plain grid, incorporating windows and doors with chequered panels emphasising the geometry of the elevation. As Bruce understands, the concept and implementation was Eileen Gray's.

'Why did you open a gallery? Surely after the success and all the publicity around the rue Lota project you were busy with commissions?'

Recalling her project work had given Miss Gray a burst of energy; remembering even the more unpleasant situations is cathartic, even cleansing. She feels alive and vital in a way she hasn't felt for too long.

'No. Not at all – I wasn't all that busy with commissions.'

Bruce finds her habit of dismissing her success endearing.

'It had long been one of my ambitions to make a business opportunity out of my early passion for lacquer furniture and the luxurious mode of décor it demanded.' She laughs. It's a natural sound, with nothing forced about it. 'There! I had years to perfect those words. I used them in my opening speech for the gallery. I've never forgotten them, so you may as well have the benefit.'

Bruce wonders might she be relenting about the interview. She's giving him a direct quote. Perhaps she'll let him write up and publish what they've discussed? He will be sensitive. She should know that about him by now, and there's nothing prurient in anything she's spoken about. It is the first time in his company she has come close to light-heartedness, much less making a joke.

'May I write that down? What you've just said – the quotation about the artistic potential of lacquer furniture?' He pushes. 'I'd like to be sure I have…remember…it accurately.' Bruce's head is spinning with the amount of information he has assimilated. While he has a good memory, he has heard and absorbed so much during the past hour that he couldn't guarantee his accuracy of recall without some form of notes.

'Well, I suppose you may.'

It's a reluctantly given permission, but it is permission. He takes out his notebook. He has marked the page with his prepared list of questions. The majority are no longer relevant as so many of them have been answered. He flicks until he comes to a blank page. In small, neat, well-spaced letters he writes what she has said. He knows he has it verbatim but he reads it back.

'Yes. That's it. That's accurate.' He senses slight admiration. He plans to make use of her more open attitude, although he cannot even begin to guess how this afternoon will end.

'Why didn't you use your own name for the gallery? You must have been well enough known for it to be an advantage?'

'I chose a masculine name because it was an indisputable fact then in Paris – despite the number of the women involved in the industry – that interior design was a man's world.'

'What a pity you couldn't be yourself.'

She gives another of those little laughs. 'That's what my friends Kathleen and Jessie said when they tried to argue me out of the name. And you should have heard Evelyn. But I didn't want to be drawn into overt feminism. Nor did I wish then, or ever since, to take up the so-called cudgels of equal opportunity.'

'So how did you come to choose that particular name?'

She shakes her head and smiles, a tight movement of her lips. This Mr Chatwin appears to be so deeply interested in every aspect of her work. He has turned out to be quite charming and so polite. A gentleman reporter – the very idea is quite the oxymoron. She suspects such men are rare. Apparently there's nothing too minor for him to question; she suspects he is a perfectionist and she approves of perfectionism. She answers: 'Jean, because it's an everyday French name, and Désert, because I never wanted to forget the experience of sleeping under the stars in the desert while Evelyn Wyld and I were in Morocco.'

What a creative and individualistic bent Miss Gray has for naming things: *Le Destin*, *Om Mani Padme Hum*, the *Pirogue* sofa and those *Sirène* chairs. And he is most certainly enjoying the rare flashes of her rather black humour. 'Did you have a grand opening?'

'Yes, I suppose, one might consider it rather grand. Such occasions were, in those days. But we didn't rely on that for business …'

By then her workshop in rue Visconti manufacturing rugs and carpets was well established and she had set up a lacquer and furniture-making operation at rue Guénégaud. Her appointment of Gabrielle Bloch to run the gallery raised many an eyebrow, but it turned out to be a stroke of diplomatic and social genius, as it drew the top echelons of Parisian bankers. By employing Loie Fuller's lover – as Gabrielle still was at the time – Eileen had hoped to further consolidate her relationship with Damia.

'We sent cards to a select list of people, inviting inspection and listing the availability of lacquer screens and furniture …' Her voice trails off. 'I think they should be in the middle drawer of my work table.' She gestures.

'May I?'

'Yes do. But be careful. That drawer is stiff.'

The long, shallow drawer reveals itself sluggishly, as though reluctant to open, and to the front right-hand side is a clear plastic folder containing several cards. Bruce picks out one: ' "Hanging lamps, sofas, mirrors and carpets, and daybeds of exotic form and deep-cushioned sofas draped in wild animal skins, such as zebra and leopard, as well as goat and sheepskins." ' Still holding the card, he compliments. 'An impressive list of stock.'

Eileen considered vulgar the blatant self-promotion of the interior designers, furniture makers and rug manufacturers of the era. In the same instinctive way that she had made her presentation to Madame Levy, she provided a stylish, seemingly low-key businesslike promotion to an advertising campaign of her services for the decoration and installation of apartments.

The *New York Times* was duly impressed with the Galerie and its contents: 'Eileen Gray's designs neither adhere to the rules established by the creators of classic periods nor attempt to achieve sensational novelty by invitation of the primitive.'

Galerie Jean Désert became the fashionable meeting place for the *beau monde*, such as the Countess de Béhague, Baron de Gunzburg and the Countess of Oxford. Although sales of the labour-intensive and costly lacquer furniture were limited, couturière Madame Elsa Schiaparelli bought a commode, a mirror frame and a black carpet; while legendary party-thrower Viscount de Noailles purchased a coiffeuse.

The abstract, modernist once-off rugs and carpets were Jean Désert's most commercially successful items. Eileen was a prolific designer, creating individualistic, abstract essays, subtle plays of lines and blocks influenced by tribal art, the overlaid rectangles of Cubism and the flat geometrical vernacular of the Dutch De Stijl group.

She gave her carpets names such as *Ulysses* – as homage to Irish writer James Joyce, whose novel of the same title was causing an international uproar; *Roquebrune, Castellar, St Tropez* – in acknowledgement of the areas she loved in the South of France; and *Tennis* in recognition of the popular sport.

'Shortly after opening the gallery I became more involved in my architectural dream – it was the direction I wanted to take. Frankly, once Jean Désert was up and running, the concept of it ceased to interest me.'

The potential of the fine-tuned contrast of the sensual, tempered by austerity of line and decoration, as employed during her refurbishment of the Levy apartment, so appealed to Eileen that she created a similar look for the 1923 Salon des Artistes Décorateurs, but it was out of key with the prevailing Art Deco style.

'The French reporters hated everything about my Monte Carlo bedroom-boudoir,' she tells Bruce. 'One reviewer described it as fitting "for the daughter of Dr Caligari in all its horrors". In case you're not familiar with Dr Caligari, it's a reference to the 1920s German silent horror film.'

Bruce is touched by her openness but confines himself to commenting, 'A reaction like that must have been devastating.'

'Initially it was, but I've always tried not to dwell on negative publicity. Or indeed, as I've said, any sort of publicity. Although my pride was somewhat salvaged when the project received favourable attention from the Dutch architect Jacobus J. P. Oud. Particularly as he asked to see more of my work.'

Chapter 19

*B*ruce knows it is a giant step to move from the familiar to the unknown. He has changed career and he is aware of the challenges it imposes. Miss Gray had made her international name with lacquer work and succeeded with interiors and furniture design involving a considerable input of lacquer pieces. After all that, she had taken the courageous decision to move into architecture.

He senses the unquenchable flame of her creative passion which, old as she is, still burns brightly. He hopes some day he too will succeed in nurturing his own passion and that it will grow to a steady flame of accomplishment rather than his usual flash of unrealised ideas and plans. Despite the structure and words of each of the features he writes being as perfect as he can make them, frequently he feels his writing lacks the passion of true commitment.

His father has courage and dedication; throughout his life he has been successful at whatever tasks he took on, be it soldier, lawyer or farmer. Despite resentment at losing exclusivity with his mother on his father's return from the war, Bruce constantly sought his approval – even, as an homage, insisting on being called by his second name, Charles, in Marlborough College. He feels he has never quite succeeded. Captain Chatwin's are big footsteps to fill.

From the time he was old enough to remember – and he is proud in his assurance that he has recall of family incidents from the age of three – he was aware of his father's bravery. It is an abiding presence within the family.

Each night after she had finished reading *The Flower Fairies* and before he snuggled down to sleep, his mother had another special ritual. After returning the book to the locker, she would pick up the silver-framed photograph and hold it close to Bruce's face. 'Now. Kiss your father goodnight,' she'd say in that way of hers that boded no argument. While he brushed the glass with his lips, disliking its cold smoothness, she dabbed at her eyes with a lace-edged handkerchief, murmuring, 'Brave, brave Charles,' before she too kissed the photo on its way back to the locker.

Bruce grasped at every opportunity to eavesdrop on what he called 'adult conversation', during which he learned more than he should.

He discovered that he had been born a beautiful baby, so beautiful that the maternity nurse commented he was 'almost too beautiful to live', but, much as he knew his mother loved him and in all likelihood had agreed with the nurse, no matter how often he asked she would never confirm it. For a while during his junior schooldays, he told any-one who would listen that he was the baby in the advertisement for Glaxo Baby Food. As a man he had learned to be more circumspect about his good looks: he knew they existed – he had only to glance in any mirror to confirm that he was extraordinarily handsome. He allowed his looks to speak for him and he used them to add to his charisma, as well as favouring blue shirts which matched the sapphire of his eyes.

It was from the various relations who came and went in his life that he learned about his father: how after a stint in the Orkneys at Scapa Flow he had served out the war as captain of a destroyer. Scapa Flow – liking the sound, Bruce rolled those two words around in his mouth before setting them free so that he could pursue the remainder of his father's war history, which involved protecting the Malta convoys and the Eastern Mediterranean fleet in Alexandria. Quite the hero, those relatives would say. And so modest too, they invariably added. The captain's heroism remained potent, like a great lurking secret within the family. He never referred to it, much less discussed those war years with his wife or sons.

Bruce wonders how the older Chatwin would handle this inter-view situation: no doubt, as always, by getting on with it.

He may as well follow in paternal footsteps. Feeling more confi-dent and surer of his ground, he asks, 'Were all your designs driven by your sense of visual creativity?' He leans forward. He is not sure what the outcome of this afternoon will be but he knows he will never forget it.

'Absolutely. They are primarily visual, creative too, but I also want them to be functional.'

Eileen Gray eases back further into her chair and raises her head a little. She is still a working artist – it is important to have Mr Chatwin realise this. To ensure he does, she has emphasised the present tense.

'Have you ever run out of ideas?'

Even as he asks, Bruce hopes she won't consider it a foolish question. He is fascinated by what he has labelled his 'marvellous' – the full-of-ideas, creative part of his being which he senses lurking in the background waiting, as it were, for a chance to come on stage. He worries about running out of ideas, and he worries equally about those same ideas coming at him with such fleeting, quicksilver speed that they defy capture. He wants to channel his 'marvellous' into writing stories that draw on the mixture of fact and fiction residing in his head. He doesn't think he wants to write a novel. It's not so much the thought of the length that puzzles him, more he doesn't quite understand the meaning of the word 'novel'.

'No, so far I haven't run out of ideas,' she says. 'And as you can see, I am still working.' There is proud asperity in her words.

'I am aware of that.'

'My mind is as full of shapes and images and materials and plans today as it was seven decades ago. I will design until the day I die.'

The longer he spends with Miss Gray the more Bruce likes her feistiness, senses the passion and dedication and recognises the driving force that propels her creativity. 'I think you're quite wonderful. It's amazing what you've accomplished.' His voice cracks with emotion.

It's a spontaneous burst of approval from Bruce's heart. He stops, opens his mouth, takes in a gust of air and looks to Miss Gray. He has done it now. How could he have spoken to her like that?

Her left eye is unblinking and he cannot read her expression.

'Sorry. Perhaps I shouldn't have said that, but I meant it.'

She opens her arms wide, palms upwards. 'Thank you,' she says. Her actions are more eloquent than any amount of words.

His sigh is one of relief. In her company he is beginning to believe he too will be able to achieve the wildest of his imaginative possibilities.

But he will have to accomplish them himself. Only he can nurture and fulfil his own creative destiny. Strange, he hadn't realised that before: it's as though the seed of creativity lying in his heart has germinated and blossomed and is now unfurling, petal after petal opening slowly. The onus is on him. There can be no more blaming his mother or father or Hugh or his wife Elizabeth, whom he hasn't ever really blamed.

Miss Gray breaks into his thoughts with, 'What, may I inquire, Mr Chatwin, are your ambitions?'

For a moment he wants to explain his fund of memories, ideas and strings of facts mixed with fiction and dreams, some thought through, more in the process, all jostling to be written down, but his mixture of caution and professionalism takes over. He laughs, opens his hands in a gesture of helplessness. 'I have too many plans and ambitions to even begin to enumerate.'

In some ways, he thinks, their attitude to creativity and life are not dissimilar. While he wouldn't dream of comparing himself to Miss Gray, he too has experienced the power of his own driving force. Against all advice – and the advice had come unwanted and unasked for from all directions – this force had driven him at the age of twenty-six to leave his position as director of the Impressionist department in Sotheby's of London.

Throughout his time in Sotheby's, he'd harboured vague thoughts of university. The catalyst that finally stirred him to academic action was his eyes. Like Miss Gray he has known the terror of failing sight. He chooses not to use the word 'breakdown' which, he'd heard, was whispered in certain circles. No, at the time it was definitely his eyes that were the problem, his only problem.

After thrilling Sotheby's and exhibiting a chameleon-like genius for taking on the necessary plumage of his various positions, quite suddenly his job lost its magic for him. He felt pressurised, burned out and experienced that dragging feeling of deteriorating health. The constant rushing from Paris and Rome to Venice and on to New York, meeting and entertaining and being entertained by clients and all that could and invariably did involve had him exhausted. Then there were the never-ending assessments of paintings and continuous organisation of a difficult series of sales.

With exhaustion came a sense of loathing – loathing for what he had become; loathing for the auction house that employed him and its silent but tacit encouragement of his behaviour. He has always been unable to explain what he hadn't rightly understood himself. Why had he developed that sudden sense of loathing? Certainly it wasn't conscience. Conscience did not trouble him. Sitting opposite Miss Gray on this murky November afternoon, the explanation comes to him haltingly, running delicately along the tracks of his mind. It has him reaching for that quote from *Hamlet*, something about being true to himself? Yes. He has it. 'To thine own self be true and it must follow, as the night the day, thou canst not then be false to any man.'

Desperately seeking some sort of an out from what he'd become and a respite from the pressure of his job, he'd manufactured a problem with his eyesight, and when he alerted the Sotheby's board of directors back in London, expecting immediate understanding and sympathy, he was ignored.

Instead of taking sick leave or requesting time off, he'd embarked on that last ridiculous dash: flying from New York into Dublin, hiring a car and driving to Donegal where he'd slept in a four-poster bed. How the four-poster bed enters into the story seems immaterial, yet he's always considered it important. To his consternation, deteriorating eyesight was no longer a fiction. It became a fact when he woke up in the middle of the night, turned on the bedside lamp and saw only a hazy amber glow.

His eye specialist asked and insisted on receiving answers to a series of probing questions. Despite his assurance that his blurring eyesight was his only predicament, Bruce ended up presenting a multiplicity of symptoms, including 'feeling brown clouds' when he looked upwards and an all-consuming urge to view 'distant horizons'. The diagnosis was tied up in words and phrases like 'pressure ... and trying to cut a dash', which he disputed.

But he had no argument when the ophthalmologist suggested giving up concentrated work for a while. With the deterioration of his eyesight, the urge to write down his stories had become all-consuming. A few weeks later he went on an extended visit to the Sudan. His stay there blessedly healed his eyes, miraculously opened his mind and got him writing on the subject of what he called the nomadic alternative. Many thousands of words later he reached the conclusion that migratory was man's natural state.

While he was excited about his nomads and Francis Wyndham's belief in their literary potential, he was still haunted by his childhood image of that scrap of skin from his grandmother's sloth and his dream of tracking down his relatives in Patagonia. On his return from the Sudan, he handed in his notice to Sotheby's. He had made somewhat of an interim decision to study Prehistoric Archaeology at Edinburgh University. By leaving Sotheby's, he reckoned he was being true to himself. Nomads, sloth and study had won out over the security and regular salary of a permanent job.

His interest in archaeology was fired by tales of André Malraux and Alexandre Dumas, and he anticipated the course would focus on the telling of ancient stories. When he'd told his wife of his plans, she'd laughed and said he'd a *Boys' Own* notion of archaeology. It was just as well he hadn't contradicted her because as usual she was right.

Elizabeth Chanler was that rare breed of special woman. Despite Ivry Guild being a first and abiding love, Elizabeth was his wife. When asked why he'd chosen her, as frequently he was – the idea of Bruce being married intrigued many people – he'd laugh and explain that when he heard her tell a story about a fly in a hermetically sealed room, he knew she was someone he could marry.

Piece by piece he sold off his personal art collection to pay university tuition fees and to support himself. Letting go of his collection made him realise he didn't have much regard for personal possessions or material things. From boyhood he had swung from being an ardent collector to a determined minimalist, glibly dispensing with collections he had spent months assembling. He changed the way he lived as frequently as he accumulated and disbanded collections. For weeks he would inhabit 'a milk white' – his words – womb of an environment before returning to living chaotically and darkly while obsessively assembling yet another collection, his life veering from calm to frenzied and back to calm. His consolation when his various collections were gone was his memories of them – the abstruse and exotic, the savage and sophisticated.

Within the opening weeks of the first term at Edinburgh, his illusions were shattered by academic discipline and what he called 'piles of old pots'.

His attitude, he realises with another quiver of identification, was similar to Eileen Gray's during her early days at the Slade.

Like her, there was a steely determination about him to succeed.

He refused to be beaten by the younger students. Difficult and against his grain as it was to be tied to regimentation, he attended fifteen lectures a week on the archaeology of the British Isles, European history and Sanskrit. In addition he wrote four essays a term. His diligence paid off. In July 1967, he was awarded the Wardrop Prize 'for the best first year's work'. Despite his initial reservations, he had become intrigued by the academic concept of archaeology, particularly what he learned of the Welsh settlement in Patagonia.

He hopes he hasn't been brusque with Miss Gray when she'd asked about his ambitions, but he's not comfortable talking about himself. 'Some day I plan to go to Patagonia,' he says. It's true. He's still chasing the ideal of that scrap of sloth skin which was lost in the upheaval of family removals and the death of his grandmother. There's nothing personal about admitting to that.

'I've always wanted to go there too.' Miss Gray points across the room. He follows the line of her arm to the framed painting on the wall. 'That's a picture I painted of Patagonia.'

He walks over to the rather surreal painting – it's a gouache, and he sees it full of possibility and promise. 'This is amazing. Did you really do this?'

She nods.

'You've captured my dream in paint ...'

As if she could. But what a compliment this young man has paid her.

'That is absolute nonsense,' she says, brushing aside his comment with a wave of her hand. 'But thank you. I shall make sure that one day you will own it.'

'That would mean a lot to me.' He thinks she will probably forget but he hopes she won't. He treasures the keepsakes of the famous.

'You have a way with words,' she says.

'Yes, and I've spent some of my happiest times writing.'

'Doing your work for the newspaper? You enjoy it?'

'No. Not that.' His answer is short and clipped enough for her to suspect that inadvertently she has touched on a sensitive point. She wishes she could see him clearly enough to make out his facial expression.

'Having a good conversation with an interesting person, like you, is the forerunner to my happy times of writing.' His tone lightens.

'I'm not all that interesting,' she demurs.

'Oh, but you are. Everything about you is.'

Unlike the majority of reporters Eileen Gray has had to endure, Mr Chatwin is sensitive to the arts: he is the kind of man to whom one would wish to bequeath a memento, and she won't forget her promise about the Patagonian painting. He has a boyish, insouciant air of wealth – most likely he's from a family with money; although whether it's old or new money she can't be sure. One can't nowadays.

She has never taken into consideration that her success was largely achieved courtesy of family money; that it is unlikely she would have succeeded in becoming an international name if she'd had to earn to buy the basics of bread and wine. Having money freed her to explore her creativity and disentangled her from having to sell her work to live; she hadn't had to meet current market requirements or design to commission. She is a woman who is used to being able to pander to her own desires. With the exceptions of the few friends, a scattering of family and those sharing her work ideology, she has paid more attention to the population of cats in Paris than to the wellbeing of the city's men, women and children. She has been extraordinarily lucky and, with her luck, extremely selfish, she supposes.

She is unable to appraise Mr Chatwin's age, but she suspects he is older than his rather immature attitude implies.

'I hope you succeed in your expectations.'

Her wish is genuine. His tentative hunger for achievement reminds her of herself, but she cannot be sure if he has the necessary determination to follow through.

For a moment he is thrown: it is such an unexpected comment, particularly for someone like Miss Gray. Nobody, not even Elizabeth, has ever asked him about his expectations, although when he had decided to go to university, he had had to answer a multitude of questions from family and friends – even the slightest of acquaintances felt free to pry. Their incredulity followed an expected path. They expounded on the ridiculousness of throwing away a promising career; the whys and hows of his marriage; wheres of money; whats of failure; and the whens of responsibility. But no one asked him about the realisation of his personal dreams.

Without ever intending to, he appears to have settled for a life of journalism. How could that have happened? It's as though journalism has sneaked up and, unbeknown to him, succeeded in capturing him. He supposes an appreciation of words, inherited from his mother and nurtured from babyhood by the stories she read him, his exceptional memory, love of books and a talent for photography, as well as Francis Wyndham's interest and assurance that he could write, had been the swaying factors in his appointment with the *Sunday Times*.

Chapter 20

*M*iss Gray bends down, reaching sideways to the floor, to drag up her shawl from where it has fallen. Her movements are clumsy as she seeks to smooth it across her lap. It would be nice to have her young gentleman visitor help her; she'd enjoy the feeling of being cosseted.

But Bruce does not offer assistance, although it would be in his nature to do so. He would like to give her the comfort of distributing the little blanket evenly over her knees, bringing it down as far as her laced shoes and tucking it around the sides of her legs to hold in the warmth of her body, the way he would have done for his grandmothers and great-aunts. By resisting his instinct, he feels he is acknowledging Miss Gray's independence and capability.

'People like you and I, we can be lonely,' she says, still fiddling with the blanket. 'Perhaps we need people more than we're willing to admit.'

It's a strange turn of subject and, from what he has learned of her, he suspects uncharacteristic. But nothing that occurs this afternoon would surprise him. Where Miss Gray is concerned, he is beyond amazement.

He isn't lonely, he wants to tell her, to assure her with a swagger of bravado. He has his work, with its all-consuming passions and enthusiasms – and, despite his reservations about journalism as a long-term career, with each new commission there is a sense of purpose and excitement, and his head is full of the stories he wants to write. He loves and respects his wife Elizabeth; his parents, his beloved mother Margharita – he still signs his letters to her 'love you to bits' – Charles, his gentle, noble father of the demanding standards and his younger brother Hugh; as well as his so-generous American in-laws; and all those friends and acquaintances, past and present, whom he meets during the course of any day. He is rich in people.

Marriage, he knows from his experience and from observing his parents' and the marriages of various friends as well as his aunts and uncles, brings instant social acceptability and it is the ultimate guarantee against loneliness. Elizabeth and he are soul mates. She understands him.

'I'm not lonely. I'm never lonely. I have a wife,' he says.

Miss Gray hasn't considered whether or not Mr Chatwin was married. But now that he is claiming ownership of a wife, she is amazed. He does not appear to be the type of man who should have a wife; nor, indeed, in her opinion, does he fit into the role of husband.

A comment is called for. 'You have?'

Her confidence that he is not husband material is a moment of epiphany, a white light of resolved certainty with images exploding from where she'd kept them buried in the dark attic of her mind. She and Mr Chatwin share more, much more, than an appreciation of various art forms.

So that's one of the reasons why she is so comfortable in his presence. Her subliminal awareness of this is probably why she hasn't asked him to leave. Just get the topic of his marriage concluded; when the delicate question of sexual orientation arises, one mustn't appear brusque.

'My wife, Elizabeth, is American. We were married in Geneseo in August '65. Geneseo in New York.'

She moves her head slightly, her nostrils widen and delicately she sniffs, as though drawing knowledge from the air. Too much unasked-for information and this surfeit of telling is rather out of character for Mr Chatwin, she thinks.

'Ah, an American bride,' she comments.

It is not as though she is racist or was reared to be so. She could not remember an incident of racism in Brownswood, although her family's attitude to the native Irish, as they referred to them, could be and usually was one of superiority. While she had an ingrained pride of her Irish heritage, as a young woman she had come to respect and identify with the sophisticated nuances of cultured Europeans. The majority of Americans she had met appeared to be more brashly mon-eyed than quietly cultured.

But education has a habit of blurring both social and sexual barriers. Being one of the first women to attend the Slade, she had first-hand experience of that.

'Did you meet your wife at university?' she asks, considering it to be the most likely explanation.

'No.' He wants to protect Elizabeth. He won't go into the details of how they met while working at Sotheby's while he was portering and she was doing secretarial work. 'Elizabeth is wonderful. I couldn't manage without her.'

'Do you have children?'

'No. But we want to.'

Bruce is uncomfortable bringing wife and marriage and, even worse, children into the space occupied by Miss Gray and him. Some topics, like some secrets, are easier to keep private than others. Out of choice, he never discusses his domestic relationship with strangers. Indeed, he is reluctant to introduce Elizabeth's name to any conversa-tion, in any company.

He has watched other men and envied the fluency with which their body language complements their words as they talk about their wives and children but he knows he does not have that ability. He can put on a good act when called upon, but he would not know how to por-tray the part of the traditional devoted English husband. He loves Elizabeth and she is a vital part of his life. She knows nothing about the role of an English husband and so has no such expectations of him. Whenever he has to acknowledge her existence, he is quick to assure how wonderful she is and how he couldn't manage without her. 'Wonderful' and 'manage' being the two words he most uses to describe his relationship with her.

As well as loving her in his own way, from the beginning he'd known she would allow him personal space, social freedom and the liberty to travel, to do what he needed to do.

One of his major reasons for marrying was to conform, to fit in. He is saddened by that awareness and the sensation of uneasiness it brings. Elizabeth deserves better. She is wonderful and he couldn't manage without her. Look at what she has accomplished with Holwell Farm, their beautiful, pink seventeenth-century home near the town of Wotton-under-Edge.

He struggles to recapture his usual control and well-honed instincts of what he thinks of as 'non-involvement'. Miss Gray was a stranger until this afternoon. Now he finds he is unnerved by the feelings of identification and understanding and the rapport he feels with her — the list could go on and on.

For much of his adult life, Bruce has practised what he terms 'impersonal'; it has allow him to keep his emotions contained, except on those occasions when his urge for physical closeness won out. Then impersonal became personal and frequently led to indiscriminate sex.

He is becoming too involved with Miss Gray. She knows him, knows who and what he is: he is aware of that from the questions she has asked, her attitude to his replies and the relaxation of her body: she has stopped fiddling with the blanket, stopped moving her fingers, stopped rotating her shoulders. There is a new calmness about her. Her acceptance is both comfortable and uncomfortable.

It would be diplomatic and wise to leave now, to make the excuse of having taken up enough of her time, to thank her for her company and her reminiscences. But he is reluctant to go: he is too drawn to the comfort of her presence.

He'll ask her about her move into architecture. Bricks and mortar could not be more impersonal.

Chapter 21

As though reading Bruce's mind, Miss Gray says, 'I would like my work to be honoured at home. It would be nice to be acknowledged by Irish architects. Their institute is in Merrion Square, one of the loveliest of Dublin's Georgian squares.'

'I'm sure you will be.'

'Well, I'm not. But next year, I believe, the Institute of British Architects are holding a retrospective of my work in the Heinz Gallery.'

'You'll come to London for the opening?'

'It's unlikely. These days I don't like to travel.'

'But you must.'

'There are few musts left to me now.'

'Perhaps the publicity of the Heinz exhibition will encourage the Irish to do something similar?'

'It would be quite wonderful, but I doubt it. In Ireland we've a saying about a prophet not being recognised in his own land.'

Sad, lonely and vulnerable, as he'd thought. To that assessment Bruce adds unacknowledged. Sometimes life can be too cruel to contemplate.

He hopes he is succeeding in covering up his sense of unease at her understanding of him. During those times in Sotheby's when he'd dropped his guard it had been to his detriment, but he had learned from his experiences. Now while on his journalism assignments, he makes sure he is accepted without condition as a reporter. No more, no less and nothing personal.

He picks up his notebook, opens it wide at a double blank page, runs the pad of his thumb along the stitching. It is a thought gathering exercise that doesn't work; he closes the notebook and sets it down on the table, its tongue of pink marker sticking out from its cover.

He looks across to Miss Gray. She is watching him. He expels air that he didn't know he was holding. He interprets her look as one of compassion, interest and understanding. No judgement there.

He frowns, relieved, willing concentration on the job at hand. 'Would I be right in saying that this functionality you mentioned earlier would particularly apply to your E.1027?' He uses the correct format for the name of the villa: E, ten, two, seven.

Intrigued by her discovery – this Mr Chatwin is quite the flashback to her contemporaries of the 1920s – Miss Gray is also impressed: he is better prepared and knows more about her work than he pretends. More than she has given him credit for.

Even the so-called experts frequently refer to the villa as E, ten, twenty-seven. Is Mr Chatwin aware of the meaning of the numbers and the lone, solitary letter?

Reminiscences scroll through her memory, a relentlessly rolling reel of film.

Concentrate, she admonishes herself. She has always been able to focus on her work; to remain in the present. Functionality, he has asked. She suspects that is something that isn't part of his life.

This rolling back to her past is disturbing. Backwards and forwards it has gone throughout the afternoon. And thoughts of architecture bring her back in time and place to Jean Badovici, the architect from Romania. She could never make up her mind about him. He was dark and intense, a sexual, tactile man with brooding eyes, a lazy smile and a quick wit. Architecture was what had drawn them together in the first place.

His early claim to fame was the complex of residential houses at Vézelay which he had designed and built; he revelled in the plaudits and publicity they received. At the time he was tipped as a man on the brink of an international future, but over the years he had expanded into more of a critic and mentor, although en route he had acquired a reputation for analysing and supporting modern architecture. He was well thought of, but he never made money from his ventures.

Even before the official opening of her gallery, Eileen had become interested in architecture: discussing its practical and esoteric concepts with Jean and approaching the process of learning in the same methodical way that she had applied to lacquering. As well as studying the work of respected architects and reading technical and theoretical books, she travelled and gained first-hand experience. She worked with Adrienne Gorska, a young Russian woman living in Paris whose clients included the Marquis Sommi Picenardi. She taught her the basics of architectural drawing and took her onto building sites where she was job architect so that Eileen could view the process for herself and gain first-hand experience of construction.

Initially Eileen refused to be impressed by Jean, but, despite herself, and thanks to his tenacity, he had grown on her. When she stopped resisting, she had fallen under his spell. At the start of their liaison, he used to gently chide her for what he called her 'English coldness'. Despite her insistence that she was Irish, he refused to change his opinion. To break through her seeming lack of emotion and response, he showered her with words and gestures of affection. He was like that then – warm and passionate, with moments of great tenderness when she felt enveloped in his love.

But at the height of his desire, when memories of Damia intruded, Eileen was unable to respond to his passion. She needed more time and patience than Jean was willing to invest. Too frequently cursing her 'remoteness', he would throw her from him, storm out and return, if he bothered to return, drunk.

'Stormy', she presumes, is the word that best described their relationship.

They were regarded as a couple by the small coterie they socialised with, as well as the wider career circle of architects, artists and designers. But they didn't live together in Paris. To anyone brave enough to ask about their domestic arrangements, she replied crisply that she liked her own space, independence and the freedom of being able to fill her time as she chose.

The truth of the matter was that she was nervous of commitment. In her own way, she did love Jean: he was funny and he made her laugh; but she didn't, she couldn't, love him with the intensity she'd felt for Damia. Eileen's feelings for her were a-once-in-a-lifetime passion, from which she had learned about the destruction of all-consuming emotions. After the breakdown of their relationship, for the remainder of her life, she was afraid to give full rein to her feelings. And yet she still craved love, affection and approbation.

She sucks in deeply and sadly, the air of the room chilly against the inside of her lips and teeth.

What is it with this Mr Chatwin? He does not appear to be intrusive – after all he'd only asked about her interest in architecture – but his innocuous question has her scrolling backwards to memories she hoped were long laid to rest. Agitated, and in a futile effort to contain her thoughts, she claps her hands to either side of her temples. She has fought against her past being raked up and brought into the present; but in spite of her efforts it is happening.

Her heart is racing and her breaths are coming in shallow gulps. She grasps the arms of the chair. Focusing, breathing shallowly, in and out through her nostrils, a reminder of Sugawara's patient attempts at composing her spirit, at calming her. She had always been nervous that this calmness of composure would be at odds with her creativity, but it hadn't arisen as she never achieved calmness. Gradually her heart rate slows and her breathing returns to normal.

'Are you all right?' His voice is edged with concern. He is squatting before her, all high-domed forehead and kindly eyes. 'Can I get you anything? Perhaps a glass of water?'

She had quite forgotten about Mr Chatwin. 'I don't want anything.' Her voice is firm. 'Thank you. Absolutely nothing. I am merely recalling the pleasure of designing and constructing my E.1027.' Architecture and design are safe subjects. But only as long as she keeps them separated from personal traumas. She can do it... She will tell the story of her villa by the sea, tell it in sequence. She doesn't believe she's ever done that.

Bruce doesn't believe her assurance – he is certain something has upset her, but he too is upset and uneasy at the turn of the afternoon's events. It is not in his remit to contradict an interview subject or even to query their answers too forcefully. He needs to settle down, keep hold of his professionalism. He looks across at the woman he is supposed to be interviewing. 'That must have been a wonderful experience.'

'Yes. It was. I succeeded in designing a house that was both modern and functional but it was also a house with a soul.' She speaks with a flourish and sounds triumphant.

'A soul?' He has never thought of a house as having a soul, but he likes the idea: the concept of a home with a soul makes sense.

'And its own pulse, too. My philosophy at the time was – and still is – that a house should be a man's shell, his extension, his growth, his spiritual glow. When I was finishing the villa, giving it the final touches, I stencilled various messages on the walls.' She sounds gleeful, like a naughty child. She is smiling rather wickedly.

He is grateful for her enthusiasm, which has him back in control, 'What sort of messages?' Grandmother Isobel's house could be described as a house full of soul, probably because it was so non-conformist, so reflective of her, her personality and her crazy possessions.

'Across the front, I wrote "*entrez lentement*" – "enter slowly". I hoped to draw visitors into the heart of the house, but I wanted it to happen gradually. Inside I put "laughter forbidden", and it guaranteed laughter. I aspired to create a talkative house – not an inanimate one. I stencilled "*invitation au voyage*" over a marine chart in the living-room. In the bathroom, I'd matching magnifying mirrors – "*madame petite et coquette*" said one, and the male equivalent teased "liking to look at the back of his neck". I enjoyed thinking out phrases and words.'

Her heavily veined hands, gnarled with arthritis, are on constant move, explaining, amplifying, seeking to clarify with arcs and circles and those sharp chopping motions that denote straight lines, squares and rectangles. Bruce understands her gestures and he follows them and their meanings, even to the extent of being able to elaborate mentally. It is as though she is bringing him to the brink of her creativity and leaving him to explore at will.

Now that her memories of E.1027 have been triggered, there is no stopping them: 'I remember that June morning in 1926 on the Côte d'Azur when it all began. I was impatient: turning the crank on the engine and driving the MG hard up that narrow, winding mountain road running from Menton to Roquebrune-Cap-Martin. I had to keep one foot on the accelerator and the other hovering over the brake. That was the summer when everyone seemed to be humming "Bye Bye Blackbird", and I sang it all the way in to the railway station.'

Bruce Chatwin, his head to one side, is watching intently, following her every word, making his own pictures, but she is no longer aware of his presence.

*

With a flourish and a squeal of tyres, she parked with the radiator of the motorcar almost touching the rough cast of the wall. As she opened the door and stepped out, her fingers plucked the keys from the dashboard. Reaching into the small back seat, she took out a rolled-up towel containing her swimsuit and bathing cap and patted briskly at her dress pockets to ensure she had her cigarette case and lighter. She never dawdled.

She had spent the past three weeks fruitlessly searching up and down the coast for a suitable site on which to build the house of her dreams, planning to couple her creativity to the architectural theory she had learned. But the right site had eluded her. Spitefully, she thought. She was thoroughly exasperated by the squandered hours chasing an objective that was beginning to look chimera-like.

The previous night, sleepless with irritation, she had risen from her bed, walked out to the balcony and stood in her pyjamas and bare feet on the wrought-iron platform, looking out to the sleepy little streets. The right site had to exist – she was sure of it, as sure as she had been about finding the right subject for *Le Destin*. But where the hell was it? She hated being thwarted. The smoke from her cigarette curled outwards and upwards.

Perhaps she needed to stand back and, instead of running ragged, nurture herself. By the time dawn's lemony light had broken in the east, she had decided to take the day off, to take time out, as Jessie would say. It wasn't until she had finished her bowl of coffee and lit her first cigarette of the morning that she decided to go for a swim and work off her surplus energy in the water.

She had even been told of a quiet, hidden cove.

Chapter 22

*A*s Eileen negotiated the railway tracks, her white shift dress was cool against her bare legs and her pale pumps shuffled dustily in the parched earth. Climbing up the opposite side of the platform, she crossed over a low stone wall and began walking along the faint pathway that wove across the top of the cliffs. She was entranced by the natural beauty and isolation of the area, the blue bowl of the sky, the silver haze out to sea and the sweep of mauve willow herbs wilting beneath smouldering ash-grey saplings. When the path fizzled out, she remained standing, gazing out along the horizon, drawn to the mesmerising sensuousness of moving water.

The River Slaney running at the back of Brownswood had the power to suspend time. She could lose herself in its flow, trance-like, find her senses tuned into the lapping sounds, rolling sight, river smell and moistness of its air on her skin. Depending on the weather, the river lapped against its banks, glided gracefully, became shrouded in silver raindrops or blanketed in snowflakes. In early morning it sparkled with life and at night it was wrapped in a veil of mystery.

Water stimulated her senses in the way of no other element.

Before beginning the hunt for the site for her house she knew it had to be located on the coast – within sight and sound of the wash of the sea. The sea was an enlargement of everything she was. Exhilarating, liberating and disturbing: she wanted its embrace.

Her bare arms were brushed by the warm, soft breeze as she clambered over the crumbling walls. Down the slope she went, skidding and slipping and sliding, fearlessly clutching at the rolled-up towel, excited at the thought of a swim, giving up on decorum and at times ending up on her bottom as she negotiated the scattered Levant pines and brushes of wild rosemary and euphorbia. Eventually, she skidded to a halt on a small natural terrace cut into the honey-coloured limestone rocks.

She laughed out loud – she was a child again, back in Brownswood, fearlessly rolling down the slope towards the river in the body of her old perambulator. When she had climbed back, pulling the perambulator behind her by a ravel of string tied to its handle, wanting to relive the thrill of danger, she was ready to repeat the exercise. Lizzie waited at the top, arms folded across her ample bosom. She grabbed hold of Eileen with one hand and confiscated the string with the other. For a moment she stood, a stocky, sturdy figure silhouetted against the house, before clipping Eileen's ears smartly. 'Don't you ever do that again,' she said. 'You could be killed.' With her head still smarting from the slap, Eileen felt embraced by waves of care and love.

She stood up gingerly, finding her feet carefully on the rocks, patting herself down. Shoes and dress ruined. Everything else, apparently, in order. Good. And she was still clutching the rolled-up towel. With feet planted wide, she lit a cigarette and gazed out to sea, feeling as though she were high on the deck of some transatlantic liner en route to New York. Below and to her left lay the almost hidden cove where she planned to spend her day. She stretched her arms high and wide, embracing sky and sea and welcoming the suffusing but rare sensation of all encompassing happiness.

And then, just above her cove, she saw it: a narrow lip glowing on the cliff face. The swim which had loomed so large on her horizon of importance was forgotten. The muscles of her stomach clenched; a shiver ran up her spine and the metronome of the waves beat ever so gently.

At last. She had found the perfect site on which to build her perfect house.

Arms wrapped around her knees, she sat among the pines watching the site, embedding every inch of it in her memory. If such a thing were possible, it was more than perfect.

The house would be designed by her, constructed to her specification and furnished with her pieces. She shivered in delicious anticipation of the architectural and design journey that lay ahead. What she didn't realise, and even if she had it wouldn't have particularly interested her, was that in time the house – her house – would become one of the most talked about and iconic houses of the twentieth century.

*

'How did the villa get its name?' Bruce asks, thinking it was probably thought up by one of the architectural and design pundits that proliferated in Europe between the World Wars, but wanting to check his facts.

So he didn't know, even though he had the right phraseology. The naming of the house was as inspired as her other titles.

Strange the way it had happened.

It was one of those infrequent days when Jean and she planned to work together. On the previous evening, wanting both time and a bed to herself, she had ignored Jean's face tightening in annoyance at having to return solo to his impoverished student-like garret. When thwarted, he could behave like a petulant child. She had used a headache as an excuse to be alone – anyway, her place didn't readily accommodate another person, certainly not someone like Jean whose untidiness was legendary and whose manner could be one of brittle authority.

After all, as she told him on several occasions, he had chosen his living accommodation. Quick as a flash he would retaliate that he hadn't the benefit of a wealthy family. He made no secret of craving her style of living. Eileen ignored his eloquent holding forth on the joys of *hotels particuliers*: the glory of their massive arched doors leading to courtyards and the synchronicity of the matching suite of three imposing build-ings leaning against each other. For Eileen, number twenty-one still held whispering echoes of Damia. And she couldn't rid herself of a feeling of disloyalty at another lover in the bed they had shared.

Eileen was up early. Before Jean came she wanted to play around with folded-out elevations arranged around a plan of each room. By doing so she hoped to get a sense of the interior space rather than just concentrating on facades and floor plans to create form. She was interested in the experience of being inside a space and focusing on materiality to produce her desired effects. It worked. She gained an awareness of the physical experience of being inside specific spaces. It was an unnerving, almost out-of-body sensation which she didn't wish to prolong.

As a distraction she began doodling her initials on the side of the elevation of the building pinned to her drawing board. Capital Es and Gs, standing tall and straight; a series of Es and Gs sloping forwards then backwards, executed with elaborate loops; followed by a grouping of variously shaped JBs, pursued by more EGs inter-linking in different ways with the JBs, but always with her initials of E and G in dominance. And because figures appealed to her more than letters she began incorporating numbers into the alphabet, using the combinations of 5 for Eileen, 7 for Gray, 10 for Jean and 2 for Badovici. At some stage in the proceedings she'd written E.1027 in the right hand bottom corner of the plan. She'd liked both the look of it and its connotation.

When Jean joined her, his attitude was the one she had labelled 'unyieldingly aloof', although he brought with him her favourite breakfast of warm croissants and apricot conserve. Sunshine streamed golden rays across her drawing board.

'How's it coming on?' he asked smiling, all white teeth and clipped moustache buckling in an arc. His question was in his most business-like voice and his nod was in the direction of the table. No sentiment this morning. That was his way of ignoring the personal aspect of the previous evening.

She had been working on the drawing of that particular elevation for several days, slowly inching forward her design but still unsure if the final outcome would match what she pictured in her head. The folded-out concept had clarified her thoughts, and now she knew she was heading in the right direction.

'It's coming along nicely, thank you.' Eileen turned away from the board to face Jean. If she admitted to even the slightest dubiousness about the elevation, he would try to take over. His insistence and her refusal would further aggravate the delicate balance of their relationship.

'Can I see?'

As he moved towards her, Eileen backed her elbows onto the drawing board, feeling like a silly young girl. Her behaviour was as ridiculous as her sister's at the time of her courtship, although Ethel's youth had excused her.

During the months and weeks before her wedding, Ethel spent long hours hunched over the bureau in the drawing room writing their initials – EG and HT – on sheets of Mama's best headed notepaper. Henry was the only gentleman who had expressed an interest in her and she was so taken with the novelty of being desired that she spent hours working on their initials, trying out all sorts of intricacies – interweaving the letters with flowers, enclosing them in hearts, encircling them in ridiculous curlicues.

Ethel's behaviour was understandable. After all she was at the age of acceptable simpering. But Eileen was a mature woman, independent and with a highly regarded career. She most certainly did not want Jean to see the results of her doodling - as though she were a lovelorn maiden.

Still holding the paper bag of croissants, he stepped closer to the drawing board. 'Have we decided on a name yet?'

He was quite obsessed with naming her house. Uncharacteristically, she did not contradict his assumption that it would be their place. Joint ownership – no less. Whenever the subject came up, as it did with increasing frequency, she would stall and shuffle her words. When he was gone and she was on her own, she would go over their conversation, analysing his every word and its meaning and regretting the weakness of her evasion.

She was no shrinking violet; she knew about refusal – hadn't her life been dictated by what she had chosen and what she had declined? She had always exercised control over her projects. Why couldn't she apply the same criteria to her personal relationships?

At that precise moment, with Jean approaching and the heady smell of fresh croissants in her nostrils, she was inspired, 'Yes, Jean, I have the name for the house.' Referring to it as 'the house' instead of 'my house' was a conscious choice on her part. 'It's going to be called the E, ten, two, seven.'

'What? *In numele lui Dumneze* what does that mean? It sounds ridiculous.' Jean's long fingers crumpled at the bag. He only called on God when he was sorely tried. 'It doesn't mean anything.'

'Oh, but it does,' Eileen assured airily with a wave of her hands. 'Can't you guess?'

'No. You'll have to tell me. I can't take the suspense.' He tried to keep his voice light but his words dripped sarcasm.

Eileen's certainty about the name felt good. She rang the small brass hand-bell on the bureau. While waiting for Louise to respond with a tray of coffee, she pulled out a lined pad from the drawer. Jean stood too close and too tight behind her: she disliked the sensation of being hemmed in.

As she wrote with a thick pencil of charcoal, she explained: 'E for Eileen; 10, the tenth letter of the alphabet, for Jean; 2 for Badovici and the 7 is for Gray.' She didn't look up when she finished; she didn't want to see his expression.

When the name E.1027 became known there was plenty of gossip about its origin. Eileen delighted in roguishly laughing off the ideas that it was an amorous gesture on her part or heralded the late emergence of a latent maternal streak – the fact that Jean was so many years her junior had provided weeks of gossip when their relationship became public knowledge.

She retained a humorously incredulous silence in the face of the rumours circulated during Gertrude Stein's soirées that the name was a calculated emasculation of Jean. By then Miss Stein was without her sting: she had lost literary credibility when she compared her writings to both James Joyce's *Ulysses* and Marcel Proust's *In Search of Lost Time*.

Jean added fuel to the flames of gossip by flouncing around Paris behaving as though the drawings and specification for the house in the Côte were his brainchild and being built with his money – which everyone knew was nonexistent.

Whenever the subject of the name was raised, and it frequently was by Jean, he showed his displeasure by sighing, muttering and clicks of annoyance. He had an obsessive streak that enabled him to go on and on about something that either displeased or enormously pleased him.

When Eileen sought to placate him, placing the flat of her palms against his chest, rationalising that surely he understood the nonsense people talked when they had a glass of champagne in their hand, he refused to see anything but his own belittlement.

Resorting to flattery, she protested that with his experience of editing *L'Architecture Vivante* and the success of the magazine throughout Europe he must realise reporters would write anything to enhance their stories and improve sales of newspapers and magazines.

No matter what words and gestures she used or how much she assured him that the name she had chosen for her house had no ulterior meaning, he would not be calmed.

Chapter 23

*B*ruce Chatwin rests back on his chair. He has willed himself back to calmness and his natural ability to project a picture of relaxed companionship is in full play. 'Did you work closely with Jean Badovici?'

'We did on some projects.'

'Including E.1027?'

'Well, yes and no.' Miss Gray clamps shut her lips.

'It's generally believed that he had considerable design input into E.1027?' The statement is asked as a tentative question. Bruce is not sure how far he can probe.

She raises her head. 'The design and construction were solely mine.'

He senses more, much more. 'Jean Badovici did a feature on you for *L'Architecture Vivante*, regarded, I understand, as the avant garde architectural magazine of the time?'

Bruce has perfected the habit of asking key questions in such a relaxed way that they appear to be without threat and his choice of words leaves the option open to correction. He is glad of the advance research he has carried out on Eileen Gray, incomplete as it had to be, due to lack of time. In the decades to come he suspects much more will be written about her and the world will laud her and her projects.

'Yes, after the completion of E.1027, Jean Badovici gave over an edition of the magazine to the house.'

'And you also featured?'

She inclines her head graciously. 'Indeed.'

Bruce's voice is quiet, gentle to the point of persuasion, his comment a question demanding an answer. 'And yet Jean Badovici had ownership of E.1027?'

'Yes.' There's no point in denying it.

'How did that come about?' It's a more probing and direct question than he wishes, but …

'That was my decision.'

Miss Gray's answer closes off any thoughts of further questions about Jean Badovici's ownership of E.1027.

In an unexpected turn, she amazes Bruce by saying, 'Let me try to explain those times and the circumstances to you.'

*

Mixed into Eileen's memories of Jean at that time are the equally potent ones of Coco Chanel, whose every move was a subject of conversation. Despite being dead for more than a year, her personality and achievements still hang spectre-like around Paris.

Jean was enchanted as much by Chanel's success as he was by the air of grandeur with which she surrounded herself. He angled for invitations to her parties and expressed annoyance at Eileen's lack of interest.

Chanel, as she was known, held court with élan, scented her home with shovelfuls of her No. 5 perfume scattered on hot coals, served premium quality champagne and soup tureens piled high with the best of caviar. As well as successful artists and the top echelons of society, her guest list included those who were not quite society but who knew how to make money. Artists, poets and authors invigorated her parties with an intellectual liveliness; the aristocracy, frozen in their own arrogance and the social bigotry of the time, added to the mood of extravagant decadence she delighted in; while the beautiful people were an endless source of gossiping froth and deliciously malicious back-stabbing.

Wealthy patrons and their dispensing of largesse were constant conversational subjects for Jean. Eileen wasn't interested in their gossip or socialising although she made it her business to know what was going on, particularly with regard to how it related to Jean. She wriggled out of Parisian social life with the excuse of needing to remain on the Côte to oversee the building of her villa.

Occasionally Jean joined her for a few days. He disliked what he labelled 'the meagreness' of the apartment she rented in Menton. Certainly it was a far cry from the Chanel luxury of *haute époque* chairs, grey satins and pale *boiseries*, but its functionality suited Eileen's purpose. Jean considered she was childishly obsessed by the villa and out of her depth to actually believe she was capable of overseeing the building of such a complex structure carved out of an even more complex site.

Jean was only regarded as successful by people on the fringes of success, but it was well known that he had a wealthy lover, and he grasped at every opportunity to live the lavish life style. E.1027 or no E.1027 and in spite of the status and interest it was garnering in the right circles, he would prefer to have Eileen with her availability of money in Paris. But he was careful to be subtle. If she got as much as a hint that he was behaving like a 'mendicant', a word she had used witheringly about an acquaintance, he knew she was capable of cutting off funding from his various schemes.

On this visit – and it was only for the weekend, he kept reminding himself, he would be pleasant at all times. 'Pleasant' was a word that Eileen used in a complimentary way to describe people she liked. For a man whose nature was to sulk if discommoded or things were not going to his liking, he had set himself a formidable task.

After listening to each detail of the progress of E.1027, he collapsed back on the bed, watching as Eileen, sitting at the neat dressing table, manicured her nails as though nothing else was more important.

He disliked everything about her life in Menton and wondered how someone with her unlimited wealth would choose to live like this, even temporarily. He hated the petty economies she insisted in pursuing with regard to their private life – although she spared no expense on her projects. He watched with rising irritation as punctiliously she wrapped a little swab of cotton wool around the pointed head of an orange stick, dipped it into a small bowl of warmed olive oil and twiddled it around until the cotton wool was completely impregnated. Anyone else in her situation would employ a manicurist.

'I hear that Chanel has signed a long term lease on Count Pillet-Will's town house.' She looked up as she spoke.

'Yes, on the rue du Fauberg St Honoré.' Jean was animated, impressed by an address on the most exclusive street in Paris, momentarily forgetting it was also the location of Galerie Jean Désert. 'How are you so well informed about what's going on in Paris?'

'I have my sources,' Eileen said, raising her eyebrows in that mock mysterious gesture he had found enchanting at the beginning of their relationship but now considered an affectation. She bent back to the manicure, removing the excess oil from the cotton wool by pressing the stick against the edge of the bowl.

When he was in Paris without her, Jean frequented nightclubs, jazz cellars, smoking dens and poker schools, but he preferred that Eileen be kept in the dark about his nocturnal activities.

'You appear to have inside information from Coco's social circle?'

Her only answer was another raise of her eyebrows.

'As well as running her businesses – and they are all successful – she knows how to enjoy herself.'

Despite inserting an undercurrent of amusement into his words, Eileen rightly suspected the remark was a dig at her. Jean considered she spent too much time working and not enough time 'philandering' – her word for what he considered to be his leisure activities.

Without comment, Eileen and stick went from finger to finger, easing back the skin of her cuticle from where it trespassed on her nails. Cuticles perfected to her satisfaction, she fanned out her hand and with a small emery board filed her nails into a perfect oval. Her movements were slow and meticulous; her attention to the task on hand was total. Jean remained silent.

The sounds of clattering, clanging and chopping came from the kitchen across the corridor where Louise was preparing their evening meal.

From outside came the bustle of footsteps along the pavements, laughter and children's voices drifting in on the last rays of sunshine, lighting up the cell-like bedroom with its white walls, bees-waxed wooden floor and rigidly square-cornered bed dressed in white linen. Filing completed, Eileen plunged her fingers into the bowl of olive oil and only then turned around to face Jean.

Certain she was about to ask him to please get off the bed, her words left him speechless..

'When the house is finished I plan to have my lawyer implement deeds of ownership. For you.'

As though drawn upwards by an invisible thread, he jerked backwards, banging his head on the brass rods of the headboard. 'The house? You mean E.1027?'

She nodded.

'You're giving it to me? But why?'

Her reasons for the gesture were complex. They had nothing to do with Jean's tattling on about the way Coco Chanel chose to dispense her largesse. They had much to do with the memory of her beloved papa, whom she thought of constantly and with great fondness. Jean's air of vulnerability, of not quite belonging, the social peddling of his artistic ability in an effort to please and to fit in reminded Eileen of her father. She believed if Papa were independently wealthy of her mother, or if he had been more her social equal, perhaps their relationship would have survived. Maybe he would not have felt the necessity to break loose from his family to try to create a new life in Italy.

Like Papa, Jean had that same air of lacking family background and roots. From being reared in Ireland, Eileen knew that ownership of land and property made a king of a man. Ireland was a place where barren patches of soil were fought over and the smallest and most meagre of rocky fields were regarded as prized possessions.

As well as a gesture of generosity, the gifting of E.1027 to Jean was an unspoken wish for continuing companionship. His accusations of her remoteness hurt. She wasn't good at emotional explanations. The older she became the worse she was at delving into feelings and debating reasons. She had lost any facility – if she ever had one – with sentimental words. Her feelings were hers, and she fought hard to keep them private. While she believed deeds spoke louder than words, still she craved the feeling of being loved and cherished and those small, caring gestures of true affection.

Unusually for him, Jean was at a loss as to how he should respond. For a few heartbeats he remained silent, but as the meaning of what she was offering sank in, he gave a little quiver of delight and swung his legs over the side of the bed. Hunkering down in front of her, his palms resting on her knees, he leaned in towards her.

Remembering the warmth of how Jean used to be, she readied herself to be gathered into his arms. His vulnerability had never been more obvious and his expression was full of pleading little-boy wonder as he looked into her eyes. 'Do you really mean it? Are you actually giving me the E.1027?' He sounded more dubious and disbelieving than she thought possible, in the circumstances.

She nodded. In view of his attitude, she was ready for affectionate gratitude. Perhaps she had hit on the right chord that would result in a warm relationship? She was filled with the conflicting emotions of love and tenderness and generosity, all jostling with her reluctance to part with E.1027. It had been her all-consuming project for so long. And it remained her *raison d'être*.

Was she mad?

No, she had thought through her offer and bargained with herself in the same way as she had as a child: if Jean visited over the weekend and if he was civil towards her and her project – she would settle for civility – she would make him a gift of E.1027. If he didn't visit and if he wasn't civil, she wouldn't. Her decision to put the house in his name was based on instinct. The idea had come to her during one of her many walks along the top of the cliffs from Menton to Roquebrune-Cap-Martin. Time, and mulling over the implications of her gesture hadn't changed her mind.

As always, Jean had journeyed by train from Paris to Nice. Eileen had met him at the station in her motorcar. So far his attitude and behaviour had been courteousness personified and without a sign of a grumble, not even his usual gripe about the interminable and uncomfortable train journey. Being a woman who had never broken a promise, she was fulfilling her side of her unspoken bargain. But there were some points she needed to make clear to him. 'Yes, I do mean it. It's my gift to you. But there are conditions.'

He looked at her sharply. He hated having any sort of restrictions imposed on him.

'What kind of conditions?'

'That you do not interfere in its completion.'

'Done.'

She waited for him to say that it would be their special place, their *pied à terre* – even better, she hoped for some kind of endorsement of their relationship. When he did neither, she added, 'And that the two of us can enjoy happy times there.'

'But of course,' he answered smoothly.

She had expected more of a reaction: if not affection, certainly gratitude. Apparently it was not to be. She would have liked to be taken in his arms, have him brush back her hair from her forehead and kiss her gently above her brow, the way he used to in their early days. When he made no gesture towards her and when she realised he wouldn't, she bent her head to the task of buffing her nails. Faster and faster she ran the block of chamois back and forth across her nails.

Without a backward glance, Jean left the bedroom to check on Louise's dinner preparations. He disliked the housekeeper as much as she disliked him and neither pretended to the contrary. No matter what was happening, mistress and servant presented a united front.

Over their meal of oven-baked fish, followed by a platter of local cheeses and wedges of melon, Jean downed most of the carafe of local wine while Eileen and he discussed the plants best suited to the soil and salty conditions of E.1027.

Chapter 24

*D*uring the three years it took to construct and complete her dream home, for most of the time Eileen remained on the Côte. Dressed in smart trouser suits and pastel silk shirts with jaunty bow ties, like a busy bee she buzzed up and down the treacherous mountain roads in her motorcar. On occasions, she was so reluctant to leave her precious project that she spent the night on site, lulled to sleep by the sound of the sea.

The villa, gouged out from the rock face, appeared to hang hazardously off the side of the cliff. The site could hardly be a more difficult one on which to build a house – Jean was right in that respect. But for Eileen the precariousness of the location was part of its charm and she refused to be daunted by any aspect of her project. Hell. She would make it work.

She paid scant attention to the experts who pointed out that the minuses outweighed the pluses of creating such a house from her design. The construction workers saw the drilling out of the rock and the laying of the foundations as a major difficulty. When they listed their many concerns she listened courteously before presenting her solution in a voice laced with English and French expletives.

Despite her lack of fluency in the language, she handled the French bureaucracy, which dominated the most basic of tasks, like a professional experienced in the art of diplomacy and negotiating. She managed the suppliers of materials with understanding and tact and dealt with both skilled and unskilled workmen with a firm but fair hand. Each time the local men involved in the construction raised difficulties about the problems of raw materials having to be wheel-barrowed from the station platform and negotiated along the bumpy surface of the narrow access laneway to the site, she joked them back to work. The workers respected her attitude of perfectionism, her acknowledgement of their skills and her attention to detail as she checked out every aspect of the building. Refusing to compromise, she ensured there was total adherence to the most minor aspects of her drawings and specifications for top quality materials.

As Eileen's home, as she thought of it, neared completion, she was concerned with little else. The excitement of anticipated possession had mellowed Jean to a confident attitude of kindly affection. And importantly for Eileen, the villa was without the ghost of Damia. She was enchanted by its architectural sympathy with both landscape and seascape. It was more than she had hoped for so passionately and planned so meticulously.

The design relied hugely on the recent miracle of reinforced concrete: standing on stilts, the villa had a roof accessible by an exterior staircase; its south window created an open façade; it had an open-plan multi-purpose living-room with a mixture of freestanding and fixed walls and horizontally oriented windows. Due to the way the building was carved out of the rock face, it embraced the physical contours of the site.

To ensure it made maximum use and took best advantage of the natural light, water and wind, Eileen took into consideration the angles of the sun and the wind. Season by season the house fitted into its environment and, equally importantly, it provided the greatest of pleasure for its inhabitants

With walls of glass, the interior looked outwards at the Mediterranean and when the villa, complete with masts, was viewed from the sea, it gave the impression of a ship lying at anchor. Sailcloth membranes protected the terrace from the sun, life preservers hung from the balcony deck and the design of the reclining chairs suggested a cruise.

On land the structure was equally impressive. By using the same wooden floors, plain white walls, shutters and lights inside and outside, the exterior terrace seamlessly converted to a second living room. The furniture was whimsical: everything that could pivot or fold up did so. At the touch of a hand, a cabinet would transform into a desk with a myriad of gadgets; lights on the headboard in one bedroom resembled a dashboard. She used chrome, celluloid, leather, wood, glass, metal and cork. No material escaped her ingenuity: she crafted a metal screen from a sifter used in flour mills and made a pivoting filing cabinet from perforated metal.

At last the building was completed to her satisfaction. With joyfully clasped hands and a beaming smile, Eileen was finally able to enjoy fulsomely rather than critically examine.

Finishing touches including the stencilled inscriptions and indications of cupboard and shelf functions were a source of humour. This playfulness was continued in her Bibendum chair, modelled on the ubiquitous Michelin tyre man. Her designs punctured the inflated seriousness of Modernism's dominant tone of muscular religiosity, and her allusive rugs added a frivolous note of comfort and intrigue, her favourite being the dark-blue *Centimètre* with its maritime machine-art flavour.

There was unsurpassed pleasure in knowing that both interior and exterior had turned out exactly as visualised. The sense of the erotic and heightened body awareness was brought to life by her use of glinting materials in the bathroom – tiled walls, folding mirrors and porcelain sink, the cool surfaces providing a respite from the Mediterranean sunshine. She believed the poverty of modern architecture stemmed from the atrophy of sensuality.

Le Destin had been a virginal design – back in 1913, despite being thirty-five years of age, she was young to creativity, relatively untouched by the joys and sorrows of personal relationships and tentatively feeling her imaginative and artistic way. The villa was a womanly design; experienced, sophisticated and symbolic of the modish mid-1920s. Into this house she poured her mature heart and soul – a heart and soul that had loved and lost and had come to recognise the power of both.

Regardless of what initially she interpreted as his lukewarm agreement, she and Jean passed many happy weeks and sometimes months on the Côte; frequently they were alone, except for Louise who always travelled with her mistress; occasionally they were joined by Eileen's sisters Ethel and Thora and their families, as well as her friends Evelyn, Jessie and Kathleen.

*

As Miss Gray talks, sketching out the story of E.1027, Bruce listens mesmerised. He has no trouble filling in gaps, visualising the situations, circumstances, scenes and players. Why, he can almost smell the scent of the mimosa …

*

Along the way of his professional path – as well as his social one – Jean had developed the ability to cultivate those he considered to be the 'right people'. One such person was Charles-Édouard Jeanneret, better known as Le Corbusier, the most famous name in European architecture and fast gaining an international reputation. If gossip of the time was to be believed, he was volubly envious and vociferously inquisitive about the construction of E.1027.

When the rumours of Le Corbusier's interest reached Eileen, she dismissed them and him with a shrug; but Jean was enthused by his interest and constantly brought his name into their conversations. Eileen was suspicious of the architect's intent and certain he had to have an ulterior motive. His book, *Vers une Architecture* – 'Towards a New Architecture' – was regarded as a bible of the times, his port-folio listed award-winning projects and his recently completed Villa Savoye at Poissy was the talk of the design community.

Wanting to protect what she saw as the purity of function of her villa, she ignored Jean's suggestions about inviting him to E.1027. The villa was her shell, her extension, a living organism with an atmosphere of solitude and concentration. Eventually Jean ignored her and issued the invitation for which Le Corbusier had been angling.

'Corbu and Vonvon are coming to stay for a few days.' Jean slid back the glass door of the living-room and stood with one foot on the terrace.

'Who?' Eileen looked up from her sketch book. She was seated at a table tucked into the corner of the decking that caught the morning sunlight, ostensibly working but in reality enjoying the epic grandeur of the Cap Martin coastline, revelling in the sense of isolation, the primal but gentle force of the breeze, the lapping water and the lack of human voices. Watching the sea was such a restorative act.

'Le Corbusier and his wife, Yvonne. Yvonne Gallis, you know?' Eileen was motionless, her chin resting on the palm of her hand. 'She's the fashion model.'

'I didn't know she was a model.' Eileen straightened up. By saying little, she sought to keep the hostility from her voice. She knew nothing about Le Corbusier's wife, but she had heard of his reputation as a misogynist and a frequenter of Paris brothels. He may have been powerful both socially and architecturally, but Eileen didn't wish to have him as a house guest. Jean knew that.

Her spirits dropped; the magic was gone from the day; but she had to remember she had gifted this house to Jean. Playing for time, she picked up her pen and doodled a decorated, curlicued X before looking up. Jean was standing in the way she had come to recognise as defensive – neck stuck out, hands across his belly, moving his weight from one foot to the other.

She hadn't competed with his admiration for Coco Chanel and she wouldn't with Le Corbusier. She breathed deeply, willing herself to calmness.

His moustache arching comically, Jean smiled crookedly. The unspoken hovered tentatively between them.

From childhood she had always hated rows and any form of unpleasantness.

He crossed the decking and sat down opposite her, his narrow face shaded in the flickering of the palm tree.

Dipping her head so that her face was partially concealed by the brim of her straw hat, she concentrated on the way the symmetry of

the palms complimented the clean lines of the building. Her peaceful-
ness was shattered and she was left with a gnawing uneasiness. Jean
was so unpredictable. He was a man who basked in the glow of other
people's successes and was overawed by their fame.

The architect and his wife arrived early the following afternoon.
'Call me Corbu and this is Vonvon,' Le Corbusier insisted, standing ram-
rod straight in disappointed anger when Eileen insisted on addressing
them as Monsieur and Madame Le Corbusier. He was scarcely in the
house before his busy eyes were blinking owlishly behind his signature
black wire-framed glasses, and his attitude was nonchalantly insouciant
as, with thumbs tucked into the waistband of his white, flannel trousers,
he examined the place as though he were a prospective buyer.

Yvonne was darkly beautiful. Wearing a slim-fitting, pale-blue
dress and a white hat with a small brim, she clutched at her handbag
and was effusive in her praise and thanks for everything.

After what she considered to be an acceptable length of time of
extending pleasantries, Eileen left her guests to Jean, who was uncorking
a second bottle of wine. She slid open the door leading to the decking and stepped outside. Spreading her hands on the rail, she looked
towards the ever-changing turquoise of the Mediterranean. Such mus-
ing usually had the power to soothe her most savage thoughts, but not
that afternoon.

Yvonne joined her and stood quietly several yards away. 'It's beautiful, isn't it?' she said, softly embracing the stretch of the Côte with a
wave of her arm. Eileen was grateful her guest didn't intrude on her
space. 'I suppose you know my husband is quite fixated on your house
and its site?' As she spoke, Yvonne remained looking out to sea; her
voice was quiet, her posture immobile. Eileen wondered had she imagined the word 'fixated'.

There was something about Le Corbusier's panther-like padding
up and down the stairs, in and out of the house and along the decking, and the unnerving way he had of looking at her, as much as his
authoritative attitude of ownership, that had Eileen on edgy guard.
His self-invention involved wearing a bow tie, a starched collar and a
bowler hat, and he had developed a rhetorical literary style combining

discipline, enthusiasm, ironic wit and moral outrage. He worked at perfecting what he considered to be an impeccable image of international success. Eileen thought of him a poseur, which in an unguarded moment Yvonne confirmed when she revealed that on his passport he listed his occupation as *homme des lettres*.

He never stopped asking questions about the construction of the house. He viewed houses as 'machines for living', whereas Eileen's focused on the sensual and livable experience of space adaptable to the needs of the occupants.

Metaphorically, he pinned Eileen against walls, creeping up on her as she sunbathed and falling into step alongside her when she took a walk. He wanted to know how the foundations were laid, how she translated her design to reality and the ratio of indoor to outdoor space. What gave her the idea for this? Where had she sourced that? What reason had she for doing something else? Did she ever consider using such and such a material? He went on and on and, after a week as her guest, he startled her by stating that he was interested in buying the site beside E.1027.

'I have such a great design in my head,' he told her, tapping at his right temple and peering at her for reaction.

Eileen was amazed at his effrontery and what she decided had to be his architectural insecurity. When she'd first heard of his interest in E.1027, she was consoled by the fact that the design of her villa challenged the modern movement that Le Corbusier championed. So he couldn't be interested in what she was doing? But no matter how she ignored it, she was aware of his simmering fury at being upstaged. She kept dismissing her analysis as the ridiculous product of an overactive imagination and she was uncomfortable at her reaction to him: the way her skin crawled when he touched her shoulders or waist. Throughout life she had avoided people she disliked, and now she had a disliked person as her house guest.

From the nurturing of her creativity, she knew there was a truth in first impressions. Perhaps, she mused, her dislike of Le Corbusier stemmed from his reputation with women and Yvonne's timidity – as well as his egotistical explanation, one evening over dinner, as to how his name had evolved: beginning from when he adopted the name of his cousin Lecor-bezier; dispensing with the Le resulted in a combination of letters similar to *corbeau* which, he explained with an expansive wave of his wine glass, suggested his crow-like profile. He finished with, 'And now all my friends call me Corbu.'

Eileen couldn't shake off the feeling that her work represented a sexual threat to the unassailable Corbu. What a ridiculous name. She refused to let it pass her lips.

As she sidestepped her guest's constant questions with vague answers, Jean could be relied on to rush in with details, to which he added their enthusiasm for Le Corbusier buying the neighbouring site. Jean was always present, shadowing his guest, offering pieces of fruit, the local newspaper or another of the endless glasses of wine the two men consumed. Jean was a heavy drinker and a messy drunk. When they were alone, she was able to exercise some control over his drinking but with Le Corbusier in residence she felt powerless.

As there was no sign of their house guests departing, Eileen decided it was time for her and Louise to take a trip to a small hotel she'd discovered in Menton.

Chapter 25

A week later on hearing that Le Corbusier and his wife had departed, Eileen arranged to return to E.1027 and Jean. She had spent her days productively: walking the promenade at Menton, thinking and planning while quietly amused by the town's prim and growing aura of Britishness; working on designs for furniture; and looking at possible sites around the mountainous area in Castellar, back from the port. She wanted to build another house which would at least match, if not better, the design success of E.1027, but this time she would draw inspiration from the land.

She had also put a lot of thought into her relationship with Jean and she felt in control as well as refreshed and creatively invigorated as she pulled up in her motorcar outside the gate leading to her villa's sloping driveway. As always she experienced a rush of affection for the squat little building nestling against the cliff. Despite her *toot toot* signal on the horn there was no sign of Jean, who usually rushed out in welcome; as with Brownswood, the pathway beyond their villa didn't lead to anything much.

Moving her shoulders up and down and her neck from side to side, she eased out the stiffness in her upper back while savouring the ruffling of the breeze and the murmur of the sea, the scents of euphorbia and wild thyme and the anticipated pleasures of being home.

Looking back down the dusty path towards the railway station, she remembered the morning she'd first walked it, the way she'd skidded down the cliff face and found her site. Maybe Jean would come out through the garden. Creep up on her. Surprise her. Usually the most minor 'human sound', as he called it, had him investigating. He was a man of great curiosity.

As there was no sign of him, she'd do the surprising.

When she came into the living area, automatically taking in the tumbled, untidy appearance that Jean created in whatever space he occupied, her eyes lighted on the far wall. She stopped breathing and stood immobile, looking from wall to wall.

The cords of her neck pulsated as she clasped and unclasped her fingers. The work satchel dropped from her shoulder with a dull thud to her feet, its long strap looping out across the floor. Her breath when it finally came was in short, sharp gasps.

The erotic violence of the large, sexually explicit murals slashed across the pristine whiteness of the walls was deranging and disturbing. On investigation, she discovered there were eight such paintings. Eight. They dominated in gashes of bright reds, yellows, greens and lines of deep black.

Stunned and outraged at the unwelcome artwork on her walls, instant as her analysis was, it was professional. The paintings were a poor facsimile of what was regarded as sub-Picasso style, in pornographic mode but much too inept, she decided, to be titillating.

It was Le Corbusier's handiwork. There was no doubt in her mind about that.

The architect and his wife may have returned to Paris but they had left behind a horrific legacy.

The windows to the terrace were open and she could see the evening sun casting Jean's shadow across the ground.

'Jean,' she called. 'Jean. Come in here. Now.'

Glass in hand, he stepped through the doorway.

Meanwhile, Louise, who had an uncanny ability to pick up on her mistress's moods, sensed the brewing stage of another row as she busied herself sorting out the dirty mess of her kitchen.

Eileen had settled on employing what she called 'reasonable' with Jean. On that occasion it took all her resources not to physically attack him while spewing out her repertoire of invectives, which had been greatly added to during the building of the villa.

'What are these?' Her voice came across in cut-glass, haughty control, as she gestured at the walls with a sweep of her arm. 'What is the meaning of this?'

'Murals. They are a gift from Corbu.'

'A gift!' She injected stage incredulity into her voice. 'How dare he. How dare he change my design.' The crisp words, dramatically spoken, were more menacing than if shouted or delivered with rage.

'He meant well.' Jean's eyes wouldn't meet hers.

She hoped he would apologise, explain extenuating circumstances, anything but his apparent compliant acceptance of the murals. From his behaviour, she wouldn't be surprised if he had held the paint pots as Le Corbusier defiled her walls, painting naked, as was his boast.

'No, he didn't mean well. And you damn well know he didn't.' Eileen's voice rose shrilly. Reasonable was forgotten. Palpitations of fury ran down her neck and back. She clenched and unclenched her fists, thudding them along the linen of her skirt. 'This defacement of my design is an act of vandalism.' She just caught herself in time to avoid saying 'of my property' – despite the legality of Jean's ownership, she still thought of the villa as hers. 'I demand you write to him insisting the murals be removed, so that the original spirit of this house can be re-established.'

'But –'

'No buts. You will do as I say. Tell him I require the reinstatement of the white of my walls.'

'I am not sure ...' By now Jean's glass was empty and he cast around for the crutch of a fill, but the bottle of wine was outside.

'Well, make sure.'

Jean had that slightly sardonic expression he employed when he wanted to enforce male superiority. If there had been a weapon to hand – a gun or a knife would do nicely – Eileen would have had no compunction about attacking him. Even in what she considered to be a justifiable rage, the knowledge that she was capable of such extreme physical violence terrified her.

Fighting to regain control, she dug her nails into the palms of her hands, taking pleasure in the rake of pain.

It was time to take refuge in both escape and silence, to exit the scene. Without looking at Jean, she picked up her satchel by its handle, straightened to her full height and went out along the terrace and into her bedroom.

Opening and closing a soundless, dry mouth, she retreated wounded and grieving, but she did so with dignity as she acknowledged the bile of the failure of their relationship. How could Jean have missed the point of the purity of E.1027? Had he no understanding of either her or what she sought to achieve with her designs?

If the living area of the villa was bad, her bedroom was worse. Her haven desecrated. The bed that should have been dressed in crisp white linen was unmade and the sheets crumpled and soiled; the wardrobe, cupboards and drawers gaped open, their contents scattered around the room; ashtrays were full to overflowing and empty wine bottles lined the walls.

She did not want to live in an environment like this. She could not. But she did not know what she could do to change the present state of affairs. She was in an impossible situation, one that appeared to be beyond her control and without apparent solution. Like the clicking gears of a motorcar, her emotions shut down until her mind was full of the nothingness of blank grey, reminiscent of the way she had felt on the afternoon when she and Mama left Brownswood.

She stepped out through the glass door to the terrace, to her exterior hideaway. With hands resting on the white rails, as they had on so many previous occasions when she'd watched what she called the silver-sandaled feet of dawn come over the horizon, she took comfort in the sympathetic gibber of the waves below while she revisited the last quarter of an hour.

Jean hadn't followed her as she had hoped he would, so there would be no apology, no making-up. He did not appreciate her villa; he was without gratitude for her gift to him of her beloved house. The pattern of her life was being repeated. No matter how hard she'd tried to persuade herself otherwise, his attitude was treading a similar path to Damia's: she had not appreciated her gift of the *Sirène* chairs either.

Eileen felt she was unlovable and knew she was unloved. What a horrid admission to have to accept.

As frequently happened, she tried to see a sliver of good – to someway justify Jean's actions. Perhaps she was being illogical? After all it was his house. 'Irrational' was the word Jean would use. 'Neurotic' was another of his descriptions of her when she disagreed with him.

Before her tears could flow, she dashed the back of her hand across her cheeks. For too long she had been fighting the sensation around Jean of treading on eggshells. Should she apologise to him for losing her temper? Absolutely not, no, she most certainly wouldn't. In the circumstances, she decided, it was he who should be apologising to her. Her loss of temper was well justified.

She had delivered an ultimatum. There was nothing further to be done until first Jean had written that letter, and second Le Corbusier had sent in his workmen to paint over the murals.

She dreaded the likely atmosphere over the coming days – Jean's bad humour, sulks and simmering anger; she hated the constant replaying of their arguments, as though picking over interminable scabs, as well as the lies and the silliness he went on with. The feeling of sickness lurking in the pit of her belly was accompanied by the now all-too-familiar shivery sensation of uncertainty.

Did she want to be with someone who drained her and who was so demanding?

Hell, she did not.

But did she want to be alone again?

No. Hell, she didn't either. In spite of his behaviour, she'd grown comfortable with the companionship of having Jean around.

But alone was better than this.

No point in not striking while the iron was hot, as Lizzie would have said.

Having made her decision, she turned away from the sea and stepped back inside. The late-afternoon sky bloomed in the window for a moment, truly the blue honey of the Mediterranean.

'Louise,' she called, stepping into the living area. 'We are leaving.'

One of the joys of Louise was her unruffled adaptability. 'Yes, Mademoiselle. When?'

'Right now. Leave everything as it is.'

'But the master –'

'He will have to manage. I will wait for you in the motorcar.' Eileen spoke crisply; her face was composed and there was a curious look in her eyes, like the timeless eyes of a statue. She was still holding her satchel, which contained a few sketches and the notes for her new villa – it was all she needed – her clothes and the creams she used to protect her complexion from the sun were easily replaceable.

*

As Miss Gray speaks, Bruce's understanding and compassion is palpable.

He writes a few scattered words in his notebook before commenting, 'It must have been difficult to walk away from Jean Badovici and your villa?' Immediately after the words leave his lips, he brings his hand to his mouth as though to cut off further comment. How could he have said that? It is not his business, but he could never imagine leaving Elizabeth and Holwell Farm.

'Yes. It was. Very difficult. But it had to be done.' Her crisp words belie her look of hurt.

*

As she drove away from E.1027 that evening, Eileen realised Brownswood had been, and would always be, her only home. Although she'd made a good job of her apartment in rue Bonparte, it was as much a workplace as a place of living. Despite the perfectly refurbished spaces she had created, she had never felt for any of them as she had for her childhood home. She'd become emotionally involved in Madame Levy's assignment and devastated at the re-orchestration of the rooms. Finally, with E.1027, she'd thought she'd succeeded. But between them, Jean and Le Corbusier had robbed her of that hope.

There was no point in trying to recreate. Brownswood and its concept of home was finally and irrevocably lost to her. It hurt more than she thought possible.

She straightened her shoulders.

She was a proven architect now, successful in her own right and less vulnerable to human foibles. She didn't know of anyone, not even Jessie, who would understand about the desecration of her walls or Jean's behaviour. Eileen wouldn't chase happiness. It was there, somewhere. Sometimes she recognised it, but frequently it felt as though it passed her going in the opposite direction.

'I believe we'll settle for Menton again,' she told Louise, tossing her hat onto the back seat of the motorcar. 'We have a new villa to build.' Truly, as Sugawara believed, work was the oil of the soul and a powerful self-healer. There was nothing like the panacea of taking on a new project and the organised daily routine and programme of work it necessitated.

Chapter 26

'Did Le Corbusier remove the murals?' Bruce asks.

A surreptitious glance at his watch shows that he's been here for almost an hour and a half. Although he is writing an occasional sentence or a few words in his notebook, the business of the interview still isn't clarified. Its outcome remains hanging in the air between them, forlorn and homeless.

Miss Gray gives a dry little laugh. 'As far as I know they're still there.' Another little laugh becomes more of a spontaneous chuckle. 'I did hear during the war – that's World War Two, of course – after they'd appropriated the house, that the Germans officers used one of them for target practice.'

Bruce digests this. What a richness of material he has accumulated.

'Did you return again to London during the Second World War?'

'No, I moved more or less permanently to the Côte. By then I'd built Tempe à Paille at Castellar. The war years were chaotic and during them I lost many of my notebooks, drawings and samples.'

'Had you further contact with Le Corbusier?' Bruce asks, certain her answer will be in the negative.

She surprises him. 'Yes, indeed, I had. He invited me to exhibit at the 1937 Exposition as part of his Pavilion des Temps Nouveaux.'

Bruce is back on red alert. 'And did you?' He can't keep the incredulity of a certain negative answer from his voice.

'Yes. Absolutely. Of course I did. I am an architect.'

'But the murals …?'

Miss Gray looks and sounds stern. 'It's surprising how time and age mellow one. Despite our differences and varying attitudes, it took me a long time to realise that what Le Corbusier and I had in common was more important than what separated us. We used similar languages and references and particularly loved the harmony of the Acropolis.'

'I see.' Bruce neither sees nor understands. And he can't resist asking, 'Were you not still angry at him?'

'Rage and hate are destructive to creativity. But of course one doesn't forget the hurt. My anger at his defacement of my property had dissipated into an acceptance of him and his work. It would have been childish and churlish to refuse to exhibit. Despite it being nearly four decades on, it was the same exposition in the same city that at the start of the century had shaped my life.'

Even before the Second World War, social awareness was undergoing change in Europe and particularly in France, where legislation passed in 1936 required employers to grant workers paid leave. With the advent of holidays for the working classes, Eileen was quick to realise that the elite who had discovered and populated the playground of the Côte d'Azur throughout the 1920s would no longer have exclusivity.

She'd always had a social conscience – you couldn't grow up in Ireland without developing one. Although for a time she had concentrated on the luxury end of the design market, she was aware of and influenced by current events. For the times, she was an impressive rarity who had developed as a Modernist but believed in design for people. She put that belief into action with her Vacation and Leisure Centre, which was in line with the policies of the Front Populaire, the alliance of left-wing movements popular during the 1930s.

Inspired by the '*Invitation au Voyage*' slogan she'd written on the walls of E.1027, she conceived her project as a seaside resort built between the main road and the sea. Her plan grouped utilities such as office, garages and a first-aid station at the back of the site, with the entertainment units, including a self-service restaurant, which in the 1930s was a radical notion, situated on the seafront and living accommodation located accessibly in between. Her project, which translated her individual experience with E.1027 into a collective one, was acknowledged as a historic breakthrough. It integrated well into Le Corbusier's global vision of bringing together housing, leisure, work and transport.

With the camping-style furniture she had designed for E.1027, she had already addressed many technical and aesthetic issues – the stools and tables were fold-up, the cabins easy to dismantle and the tents could be erected by one person and were light enough to be carried on a motorcycle or in a motorcar.

The woman who had catered to the luxurious end of *le tout Paris* made the transition from sumptuous to institutional designs with apparent ease.

Most of the projects exhibited in Le Corbusier's pavilion were designed collectively by groups such as CIAM (Congrès International d'Architecture Modernes). In striking contrast, Eileen Gray's centre had its own autonomy. Despite being presented as an individual initiative, it became swallowed up by the powerful Le Corbusier rhetorical machine. To add insult to injury, her name on the promotional material was mis-spelt. But worst of all, the project was never considered for development.

'Your forgiveness of Le Corbusier is very magnanimous,' Bruce comments.

She shakes her head in wry amusement and replies, 'In the circumstances, not at all.'

If only Mr Chatwin knew the full story of the thorniness of her relationship with Le Corbusier. How he wasn't satisfied until he'd constructed his prefabricated cabana and hostel building that loomed obtrusively and brooded menacingly over her beloved E.1027. It seemed rough justice when he'd died from a drowning accident that her villa was probably the last thing he saw, and she was not hypocritical enough to grieve for him.

'What circumstances?'

'It doesn't matter now.' And it didn't, she would never go into it. 'He wrote me a letter – I think it's in the folder in the top drawer of the desk.' She indicates a corner near the window.

Bruce opens the drawer, takes out the folder and brings it to her.

'You may read it.' Being able to trust is a good feeling and this is a man one feels one can trust. Perhaps, after all, there's something in the Talking Cure. Imagine it has taken her all these years to come to this conclusion.

Bruce opens the folder. It's the second letter, handwritten in a black scrawl on quality white vellum.

Miss Gray's eyes are closed as she recites: 'A rare spirit which has given the modern furniture and installation such a dignified, charming and witty shape.'

'Word perfect,' Bruce compliments.

She inclines her head. 'That's what he said about my work. I liked my houses to reflect humour, fantasy and an ability to play with non-sense. Le Corbusier recognised that.'

The years have not fulfilled her girlish dreams. How optimistically and effervescently she had announced to her father on that sunny Italian beach that she would be an artist. She has known success, rejection, obliteration and now, rediscovery. If time has taken from her certain illusions, it has left richer realities in its stead. She knows that and feels she is gradually adjusting to the new image of herself.

She has not turned out to be the heroine of her dreams – whoever that person was – but she is herself. The relief of acceptance is all-encompassing.

'You may write about me, if you still wish. You may have your interview,' she tells Bruce. There is fragile nobility in her tone.

Bruce jerks upwards, astounded. 'Thank you,' he says.

He is jubilant. The joy of her permission is profound. After her determined refusal, he actually has Miss Gray's consent to write up his interview with her for the *Sunday Times* Magazine. Has he heard right? He is unsure of how to reply, afraid to break the delicate fabric of her permission. Part of him rejoices that he doesn't have to return empty-handed to Magnus Linklater. But as soon as he has absorbed the happy implications of that, another part of him, the larger part, worries that by publishing what seems special and private, he may be taking advantage of Miss Gray.

She is so old. Despite being a working artist and her plucky air of being in control, he has seen her emotional fragility. For nearly two hours he has watched her drift backwards to the unceasing pull of the past and the unravelling of memories that had nowhere to go. And in those drifts he had caught her at the point of disentanglement. Since his first pull on the bell outside the black gate of number twenty-one, he has worked towards this moment; now that he has achieved his objective he's uncertain.

'Are you sure about the interview?' he asks.

'Yes. Absolutely. Haven't I said so? Have you all the information you require?' She sits busily in the last stages of what to her has become an interview project, tidying her blanket, moving her feet, ignoring the protesting meow of the cat. He wonders what has changed her mind.

He won't ask.

Will she want to see his article before it's published? Probably not – it's the more insecure interview subjects that demand that. He is privileged by her generosity and rich with the information she has shared.

Now that the interview is over, he is exhausted – his joints ache, his body craves sleep, but in the course of this afternoon he has found a strange sort of peace and a new sense of purpose – attributes he didn't know he was missing until he discovered them deep within. He is subdued in the elation of believing he can make his dreams come true.

He should go. Miss Gray must be tired too and he's taken up enough of her time.

He'll return to his hotel and put down the facts on paper – many of which will require verification when he returns to London. But his impressions of Miss Gray will be with him forever.

Already he is beginning to envisage the finished piece, his opening, the development and ending. It will be the best he's ever written. He knows its possibilities and he'll make sure of its perfection.

Elizabeth will be pleased. He will make things up to her, he truly will.

'Yes, I have everything I need,' he tells Miss Gray. 'And thank you.'

He comes to stand in front of her, hunkers down and takes her two hands in his. The contact is brief, her hands are still so cold and his so warm. Soft light from the side lamp folds gently around him.

She looks at him. They are on a level. Her one eye makes her expression inscrutable. No matter how she feels about publicity, she could not be the reason why this beautiful young man returns empty-handed to his newspaper: he is a brave soul in a difficult world; life will never be easy for him.

She will probably regret giving him permission to publish. She is sure she will. So why has she relented? She doesn't have to query for long. She knows. In his company the ghosts of November were less and the memories of the past clarified with the bitter sweetness of acceptance and forgiveness.

She lifts the little bell from where it is tucked into the seat cushion of the chair. Its handle is warm from her body. Now she remembers placing it there before Mr Chatwin's arrival.

Its clapper clanks against the sides of brass. There's finality rather than security about its sound.

Louise appears within seconds.

'Goodbye,' Bruce says from the doorway. 'And thank you again, Miss Gray. It has been a privilege. Perhaps we'll meet in London or, perhaps, I may visit another time?'

She doesn't answer.

Louise accompanies him to the door. Methuselah, seeming even more muffled and bent, escorts him back across the courtyard. Dark and cloaked in fog, punctuated by hazy points of light, the gloom of the evening is complete in every crack and crevasse as rain falls obliquely against the lamplight. Between the Vionnet and Gray interviews he has spent a productive weekend.

As he reaches the high gate he stops and turns around. 'Wait a moment,' he calls to the old man.

*

As Louise tends to the fire, she knows better than to ask Mademoiselle Gray anything about the strangely beautiful young man who stayed for such a long time. But her mistress is not her usual reticent self. Not that usual closed-over way she can be at the intrusion of strangers into their lives.

'Mr Chatwin is a reporter,' she says.

'Is he?'

'Yes. From a prestigious English Sunday paper.'

Louise continues noisily shovelling nuggets of coal from the scuttle and scattering them on the fire.

'I was being interviewed. That's why he was here.'

'You enjoyed his company.' Louise's back is towards her and her voice is muffled as she uses brush and shovel to clear the coal dust from the hearth. Instead of looking worn out and agitated, Miss Gray appears to have had a pleasant time and these days there are few enough such occasions. 'A nice cup of tea and some bread and butter?' she is saying as the doorbell to the apartment rings.

Wiping her hands on her apron, she opens the door to Mr Chatwin. He must have forgotten something.

'May I see Miss Gray again, just for a moment?'

Louise hesitates. Old habits die hard. From as far back as the days of *Le Destin* she has been skilled at protecting her mistress. But this young man is different …

'Please,' he asks. 'It is urgent. I need to tell her something. Don't worry. She'll be happy with it.'

Louise nods. Bruce steps inside. He moves quickly down the corridor and opens the door. He returns within a few seconds, smiles at Louise, turns up the collar of his jacket and sets off across the courtyard again to where the old man waits to lock the heavy gate after him.

From a career point of view, he may have shot himself in the foot. He can imagine Magnus Linklater's sarcastic comments and expression of smugness at having his doubts confirmed about young Chatwin's journalistic ability. As he steps out to rue Bonaparte, he can hear the gravelly voice: 'Just as I expected. Going all the way to Paris and coming back without the interview.'

There is no doubt in Bruce's mind that he has made the right decision.

When Eileen Gray died in 1976, she bequeathed her gouache of Patagonia to Bruce Chatwin. *In Patagonia* was published in 1977. It established Bruce Chatwin's international reputation as a travel writer.

Book Club Discussion Questions on *The Interview*

1. Patricia O'Reilly has said that Eileen Gray is the "guiding spirit" of The Interview. What do you think she means? Do you consider Gray to be this spirit?

2. Do you think that Eileen Gray is the "heroine" of her own life? What, in fact, does it mean to be the "heroine" of a novel?

3. How convincingly does Patricia write about Gray's dedication to her work and her sense of loss, isolation and loneliness?

4. How convincingly does Patricia write about Bruce Chatwin? Build a character profile of him.

5. What do you think of Eileen's relationships with: her mother, father, siblings; her housekeeper, Louise Dany; Damia and Jean Badovici? Was she a good daughter to her mother? Is she pleased or resentful of Louise's dedication to her? Are we meant to like the people in Eileen's life? Are you surprised at Eileen's reaction throughout the book to Bruce Chatwin?

6. Talk about the ways in which the various people in Eileen's life influence her or ...the various people in Eileen's life influence her or do not influence her.

7. Many experts on Eileen Gray believe Damia had too much influence on her. More say that Damia was the love of her life. Do you consider it was a good relationship for Eileen? If so, why? If not, elaborate.

8.   The Interview ponders Eileen's and Bruce's attitudes to beauty and art. Why is art so important to the human soul? What are its consolations ... and what are its dangers? Can we become trapped in our admiration?

9.   What does the future holds for Bruce Chatwin? Why do you think Patricia left the book's conclusion open as to what happens to his interview?

10. If you were to cut portions of the book, where would you make those cuts?